CONGO ICE

ALSO BY BRENT TOWNS

Team Reaper Thrillers

Fear the Reaper Series

The MI6 Files

Talon Series

Mark Hayes Series

Dave Nash Thrillers

Treasure Series

<u>The Gods of War Series</u>

Genocide

CONGO ICE

THE GODS OF WAR
BOOK 2

BRENT TOWNS

ROUGH
EDGES
PRESS

Rough Edges Press
An Imprint of Wolfpack Publishing
1707 E. Diana Street
Tampa, FL 33610

roughedgespress.com

Paperback ISBN 978-1-68549-359-2
eBook ISBN 978-1-68549-358-5
LCCN 2024938886

CONGO ICE

CONGOICE

PROLOGUE

MI6 INTERROGATION SITE, LONDON

"WELCOME BACK, GENTLEMEN. ARE YOU ALL READY FOR ANOTHER day?"

I stared at Charles German. He was part of the Parliament Intelligence committee interrogating Knocker and me about our recent activities, and like a lot of politicians, they smelled blood in the water.

My name is Kane. John Kane. People call me Reaper because of the tattoo on my back. Beside me sat Raymond Jensen, Knocker to people who liked him, numerous other names for those who didn't.

We were both around the same age, same build, and even went unshaven, although it was trimmed neat. He was former SAS, me, former Recon Marine. We'd both served together in times gone past and became firm friends.

The three people opposite us had changed their clothes from yesterday. The two men, Charles German and Jack Holland, still wore suits, but these were freshly pressed, and their creases stood out. Christine Ryan, on the other hand, now wore a royal blue dress.

All three were in their forties, Christine Ryan the most outwardly disdainful toward us. The other two I wouldn't have trusted either. I'm not sure if they just hated us or were envious of what we had achieved. Either way, they were openly hostile to both Knocker and myself.

Previously I noted that they were the new age type of politician. Christine Ryan, though, had been in our shoes as a field operative before. It still didn't make her any less hostile.

They did, however, give us a reprieve from the day before. A change of venue. Instead of a cold, stainless steel table sitting acting as the barrier between us in the stark white room, we'd moved to what resembled a boardroom with a wooden table. I stared at the third chair beside me. "Expecting someone else?"

Holland opened his mouth to speak when the door to the room opened and Holly Smith entered. "Sorry I'm late. Traffic."

"Good of you to join us," Christine Ryan said caustically.

"Yes, ma'am."

"Looks like someone had their grumpy pills this morning," Knocker whispered, but his words were still audible.

Christine Ryan glared at him.

"Can we at least get started?" Holland asked.

"Good to see you, Holly," I said.

"You, too, John. Raymond." She nodded to each of us before sitting in the spare seat and smoothing her skirt.

"Holly. You been thrown under the bus too by the head shed?"

"Are we done?" asked German.

We remained silent.

German opened a file and said, "So, after the debriefing yesterday, we ascertained a few things. Now we move on to the Congo incident."

"I'd call it a fucking shit storm," Knocker growled. "It was worse than fucking Syria, if that is at all possible."

Christine Ryan said, "Miss Smith, everything seemed to start with Karachi. Can you give us a brief explanation about the intelligence you were acting upon and why—I suppose God himself only knows—why you chose Mr. Kane and Mr. Jensen for the operation?"

"Have you seen their records?" Holly asked, astounded that the question had been verbalized.

"Unfortunately, yes."

"Then you know why."

"Please answer the question."

Holly nodded. "We received intel that there was a shipment of illegal arms transiting Karachi. We needed someone to have a look and destroy them on-site. These guys were the obvious choice seeing as they were cooling their heels with MI6. I ran it past Brian, and he told me, my op, run it how I want. So, I put together a team and gathered intel before we went."

"I see. What about rules of engagement?"

The woman looked at me, her coal-black eyes burning holes in my exterior. "We use our rules, ma'am."

"What might they be, Mr. Kane?"

"Kill them before they kill you."

Charles German cleared his throat and said, "All right, let's begin. Start with Karachi."

I shook my head. "You'll see a side note in the file you have."

German looked, found it, then raised his head. His eyes were full of confusion.

"What does it say?" I asked him. "Just so the others can hear."

"Convoy of Death."

CONVOY OF DEATH

Unbeknown to us, it had actually started in the Democratic Republic of the Congo. Rebels were rising up against the current government and driving hard toward the capital. The rebel army had all but surrounded Kinshasa, and thousands of civilians had been displaced. This had forced the UN to start driving food convoys into the jungle to feed the masses at several camps.

The rebels were fighting for wealth. They claimed the government was reaping the rewards of the county's mining industry and keeping most of it for themselves while many went hungry. Also, that western nations were raping their country and their women as well.

They were led by a former army general, Edo Wissa. When he broke away, he took many with him, and from there, his numbers only grew. On the other side of the coin, you had Arthur Kayembe. The President of the DRC for the past ten years and one of the richest men who lived there.

The UN came into the DRC in the middle of the conflict to support the displaced civilians. Peacekeepers were also deployed to protect the camps and routes utilized by the aid convoys. Most of the peacekeepers were French with a smattering of other forces. And while they tried to keep the routes secure, they didn't ride shotgun with the trucks.

This was where one of the convoys ran into trouble and everything kind of began. The aid convoy was commanded by a former French soldier, Didier Gallas. He had been a Legionnaire serving in North Africa, Mali, and even Afghanistan. Eventually he'd had enough of the killing and thus ended a decorated career, and he went into helping others. UN aid convoys fed that need.

The narrow road they traveled was wet from one of the many storms that passed through the thick jungle.

The camp they were bound for wasn't far from the Congo River. The road they used was one that also accessed a local diamond mine, running almost past its front gate, so to speak. The *Kirefu Shimu*, or Deep Hole, was run by a Belgian mining company.

But not this day. As the lead truck approached, four men dressed in jungle fatigues stepped into the middle of the road in front of a roadblock. The one in the center held up a hand for them to stop.

All four men were armed with what looked to be AK-12s. Gallas frowned from where he sat in the passenger seat and reached for the radio transmitter. "This is Truck One, everybody stop. I repeat, everybody stop."

All seven trucks ground to a halt, gears grating and air brakes whooshing. Gallas sat there and stared at the men in front of his truck. The driver said, "Who are these men?"

"I do not know, Hugo. But I do not like what they are doing."

Gallas climbed down from the truck cab and slowly walked around to the front where the men waited. "What is going on? We need to get through to the camp with the aid we are carrying."

"You will have to go back, Frenchy," the man in the center said. "The road is closed."

Gallas couldn't help but recognize the accent. It was Russian. "Why is the road closed?"

"Because it is."

"But we need to get to the camp. The supplies we have are vital."

"So?"

Gallas stared at the man. "What are Russian mercenaries doing here anyway?"

The man's demeanor changed. Instead of shrugging it off, he became angry. He drew his MP-443 Grach handgun and pointed it at Gallas's chest.

The Frenchman raised his hands and backed up a couple of steps. "Hold it. What are you doing?"

"Get back in the fucking truck and turn around."

Hugo opened his door and climbed down, walking forward to stand beside Gallas. "What are you doing?"

The Russian with the drawn handgun turned his gaze to Hugo and adjusted his aim. Then he fired.

The bullet from the Grach punched into Hugo's chest. The French driver stopped suddenly, his mouth agape in shock. He staggered and then dropped to his knees.

"No!" Gallas cried out. He ran to his driver and friend's side. Dropping beside him, he took Hugo in his arms. "What have you done? You murderer."

Gallas looked down at his friend and then back up at the shooter. "You will go to prison for this. Once word gets back to the UN."

The man nodded. Then he said something to his friend. They started toward the trucks. Gallas looked concerned. "What are they doing? What did you say to them?"

The Russian raised his weapon. "I said kill them all."

Then he shot Gallas in the head, and the slaughter began.

CHAPTER 1

I TOSSED MY DUFFEL ON THE FLOOR AND SAID, "THIS LOOKS something like Knocker would live in."

We were on the first floor of a three-floor building in a less than salubrious part of Karachi in Pakistan. The whole floor was open plan, concrete pillars holding up the floor above in regular, uniform rows. There was garbage strewn around everywhere, complementing the inch-thick dirt and dust on the floor.

"Fuck you, Reaper," he shot back at me.

I grinned as the rest of the team came in. Holly Smith was followed by Ben Chambers, Lynda Manning, Julia Firth, and Luke Chapman. All had their own personal job on the team. Holly called back over her shoulder. "Okay, let's get set up. I want this hide operational in twenty minutes."

"If her bathroom breaks are any indication, Lynda will need an hour," Ben Chambers said.

Lynda turned, sucked her middle finger, and gave him the bird. "Sit on that and spin, asshole."

Lynda was the computer tech on our team. She was late twenties with long brown hair and an athletic build. She was a runner and practiced yoga daily. Whereas Ben Chambers, our surveillance guru, was built a little on the larger side. Not fat, but could easily run that way if pushed by food.

"Says the guy who, when he has a shit of a morning, takes a fucking book," Julia Firth growled, sticking up for her friend.

"It helps me relax. That way it just slides out."

Julia wrinkled her nose, squishing her freckles together. "Too much information, sunshine."

She let her long red hair down and then tidied it into a neat ponytail. She dug into her pack and took out some batteries and comms equipment.

Luke Chapman was just there for added security and anything else that needed doing, including driving. Unlike Julia, he had black hair but was built in the whipcord way she was of a lightweight boxer. Both were in their early thirties.

Knocker and I checked our weapons. Two Heckler and Koch 433s. We also carried the Heckler and Koch P30 handgun.

Placing them aside, we each checked out our other kit. NVGs, Body armor, Under Armour Octane Wrap Sunglasses, and several other items.

Julia approached us and handed each a small rechargeable bank with our earwigs inside. "Don't lose them."

Knocker and I placed them in our pockets. Then, for the next thirty minutes, we loaded magazines for the 433 and the P30.

Holly came over to us and said, "You two take a little drive this afternoon and have a look at the port and the target."

I nodded. "How long is the ship in port for?"

"It sails tomorrow."

She passed me a photo of the ship's stern. The name of

the vessel was *Andromeda*. Holly gave me another piece of paper. This one was a map of the port. "The ship is here at its own berth."

"Do we know where the weapons came from?" Knocker asked.

"No idea," Holly replied. "Just do your preliminaries so you can plan for tonight."

"Yes, ma'am."

"Wait one moment," German said. "Where did the weapons come from?"

Holly said, "We eventually ascertained that the bulk of them had come from Russia and more from Iran."

He nodded slowly. "I see."

German stared at me, waiting for me to continue.

Later that day, Knocker took our battered, faded yellow van and went to the port. We sat there for an hour looking through a chain mesh fence, watching the ship. We counted armed guards and worked out the best way on deck was by one of the hawsers. With Chambers acting as overwatch we figured we'd have no more problems than usual getting aboard the ship. Finding the shipping container the arms were in might prove more difficult.

"How the fuck are we meant to find the correct twenty-foot box among all of that, Reaper?" Knocker asked.

"We just have to get lucky with the number," I replied.

"Hey, look at this." He passed me the binoculars. "Check out the pillock at the gangplank."

I took the binoculars and put them up to my eyes. "What am I looking at?"

"His weapon."

I focused my scrutiny on the gun and recognized it right away. It was a PP-19-01 Vityaz. "Russian Special Forces."

"Bingo," Knocker replied, taking photos. "Now, why do you figure that Russian special operators are guarding illegal arms?"

"What I'd like to know is where they're going."

"I don't like it. Something about the whole thing smells."

I nodded in agreement. "Come on, let's get out of here."

———

Holly glanced over the pictures before looking back up. "Why would Russian Special Forces be babysitting a shipment of illegal arms?"

"My question exactly," Knocker replied.

"Where are they going?" I asked Holly.

"We don't know. We just got the intel they were onboard. I took it because I thought it would be an easy op. Now this."

"Do you want to abort?" I asked her.

Holly shook her head. "No. We've come this far. Lynda, do you have a moment?"

"Ma'am?"

She hurried over to where we stood, giving Knocker a sly glance. He gave her one in return. Of course, they'd been sleeping together since the op began. I believe the Brits call it shagging. "Take these pictures and see if you can identify the men in them."

"Yes, ma'am."

I said, "Our biggest problem is going to be finding the shipping containers that the weapons are in."

"We have numbers, but without a manifest, we're not sure where they are."

"I can try hacking their system," Lynda said.

"You can do that?" I asked.

"No, but I can try."

"Ben will be with you, operating the drone over the ship so he can direct you," Holly said. "He'll be in the van."

"We'll need a five-minute diversion," I said to Holly. "Just long enough for us to get through the fence and up the bow hawser."

"I guess we could knock out the power to the dock. That'll take down the lights."

"It might work," Knocker said. "Failing that, we'll just shoot the guard on the gangplank."

Chambers came over and held out his hand. In his palm sat three micro cameras. "Take these and place them in strategic spots so I can get better coverage."

I put them in my pocket. "Anything else?"

"Not as yet."

A couple of hours later, just before we were to leave, Lynda approached Holly and I and said, "If you want to know where they are going, you'll need to get the information from the bridge."

"How are we meant to do that?" I asked.

"Middle of the night, it should be vacant. I also found schematics of the ship and there is a stairwell you can use which will take you straight up onto the bridge."

"I'll make that call when we're aboard."

Holly nodded. "Fine. The weapons take priority. The intel about their destination will be secondary. Do you have anything on the men in the photos?"

"Nikodim Putilov and Renat Timoshenko. Former Russian Special Forces, both dead. Helicopter crash in Syria."

"Shit, here we go again."

Holly looked at me. "You don't know that, John."

"Don't know what?" Knocker asked.

I said, "Our Russians are dead guys who went down in a helicopter in Syria."

"Fucking bollocks. I knew I had a bad feeling for a reason."

"Mind letting me in on the secret?" Lynda asked.

"Gods of War. Clandestine shit of the next level run by and staffed by fucking zombies."

"Zombies?"

"Yeah, dead people."

"You don't know that?" Holly said.

"I guess we'll find out," I said.

Knocker and I finished with our equipment and then went to work.

"Kill the power," I said as I waited behind Knocker.

"Roger that," Lynda said, and then all the lights around the docks and the surrounding area went dark.

"You've got five minutes, Ghost One."

Knocker was already making a hole in the fence while I could hear confused voices coming from the ship and dock. It took Knocker thirty seconds to get a hole big enough for us to pass through.

Chambers was in the van out of sight, controlling the small drone overhead. As we passed through the fence, I heard him say, "Ghost One, you are clear to Point Bravo. Our friends are just milling around at this time."

Point Bravo was the hawser at the bow of the ship. "Roger that. Proceeding to Point Bravo."

We hurried through the darkness to the hawser. From there, we climbed the thick rope and slipped onto the deck. Knocker and I crouched down and waited for the all-clear.

The power came back on.

"Ghost Team, you have three guards roaming the deck and I have a blind spot to your southeast."

We moved forward and Chambers said, "Set up a camera there."

I reached into my pocket and placed the camera as suggested. "How's that?"

"Good signal, Ghost One."

We started searching for the number of the shipment we sought, but it quickly became evident that it was like looking for a needle in a metal haystack. I said to Knocker, "This is fucking hopeless."

"Good thing I brought extra then," he replied.

I nodded. "Bravo One, request permission to go to plan B."

"Permission granted," Holly replied.

"What was plan B?" Christine Ryan interjected.

"We couldn't find the weapons which meant if we left it at that, then they would continue on," Holly told her. "We couldn't let that happen."

"So, what did you do, Mr. Kane?"

"We took extra explosives."

"I see."

We started to creep toward the central part of the *Andromeda* when Chambers said, "Hold. Danger close."

Going to our knees, we waited in the darkness for the threat to move on. But they didn't, they kept coming. Chambers said, "X-Ray closing your position. Five meters."

I grabbed my knife, letting my 433 hang by its strap. My body had turned into a coiled spring as I waited for the confrontation.

"Three meters."

My heart thumped in my chest.

"One meter."

I tensed.

"Now."

Coming up from my crouching position, my left hand clamped over the guard's mouth while my right hand drove the knife home, through his back, up between his ribs and into the beating heart.

I then withdrew the weapon and slashed it across his

throat, making doubly sure, before lowering the dead Russian to the deck.

We dragged him into the dark gap between containers and kept going. Minutes later, we figured we were in the right position, and Knocker set the explosives. "We've got thirty minutes, Reaper."

"Ghost One, I need a situation report," Holly Smith said. "What are your intentions?"

I looked at Knocker, who nodded. "Bravo One, charges are set, proceeding to secondary target."

"Keep in mind you only have thirty minutes."

"Too well aware of that, Bravo One."

"Okay, good luck."

We made for the stairwell which led up to the bridge. Reaching it, I placed another camera facing the entrance so Chambers could watch our six. Heading up, we'd made it halfway before our eyes in the sky said, "Ghost One, you're about to have a problem. One of the guards has found—yes, he's reacted as expected. He found your dead guy."

"Copy. Keep us updated."

We continued climbing until reaching the bridge. Securing it, we locked one entry point while leaving the other open. Then we started looking around.

"These guys are starting to get anxious, Ghost One. Wait, you have a shooter coming your way."

"Roger that."

"Got it," Knocker said. He flicked through the papers he had, shining his small flashlight on them. "Okay, Reaper, the ship is headed for the DRC."

"Russian support for the coup of the government?" I said out loud.

Holly, who had been listening in, said, "There has been no open support for either side."

"Well, someone is supporting them," I replied.

"Yeah, I think we fucking know who," Knocker stated.

I looked at my watch. "Time to go, Monte."

The gunman Chambers had warned them about appeared at the locked hatch onto the bridge. He saw them inside through the porthole and opened fire.

"Definitely time to go, Reaper," Knocker said as he ducked low, bullets hammering through the broken glass.

We started back down the stairs to the main deck.

"Ghost One, you have an X-Ray coming up the back way."

I brought up the suppressed 433, and as soon as he appeared, I opened fire. The bullets caught him in the chest, and he fell backward down the stairs to the first landing.

We continued descending until reaching the deck and stepped out of the stairwell.

"X-Ray on your left, Ghost One."

The voice was urgent, and instead of turning to face the threat, I ducked back just as gunfire ripped through the air. Knocker said, "That was close. You almost were a ghost."

"Shut up," I growled and counted to three in my head.

I stepped around from cover and opened fire at the shooter. Again, a Russian operator fell.

"Knocker, press forward to the side where the gangplank is. We need to get the fuck off."

"Ghost One, you have two more X-Rays closing in on your six. Another to your—"

Bullets started smashing into the containers all around us. "Contact left."

I opened fire, and Knocker followed suit. The shooter to our left fell to the deck, his back arched in pain. More bullets cut through the air, and Knocker cried out, "Contact rear. Fuck."

I swung my weapon around. By the time I'd made the turn, Knocker already had one Russian down. The second disappeared behind a stack of shipping containers. I took cover and looked at the luminous face of my watch. "Knocker, we're running out of time."

"Tell me about it," he threw back at me while firing another burst. "These Russian pricks are all over the world lately."

"Keep falling back."

Then, as we went to move, I heard something bounce on the deck. I looked down and my heart stopped. "Grenade!"

We threw ourselves flat on the deck behind a container. The grenade detonated almost immediately when we hit, and it made a deafening sound. In my earwig I could hear Holly calling to us, but as I tried to speak, nothing came out. I was too busy trying to draw breath. I rolled onto my back and willed myself to my feet.

My bell had been rung good and I shook my head to clear the fog from my brain. I looked at Knocker. "Are you alright?"

"Shit, Reaper, thank fuck you saw that thing."

I dragged him to his feet. "Let's move."

The shooting had stopped, and we started moving again toward the gangplank. A Russian guard appeared in front of us, and I had enough time to bring my 433 into play.

He hit the deck with a handful of rounds in him, and I stepped over his still-twitching body as I pressed forward. Ahead of us, I could see our destination, and after one more step, things changed. We started taking fire from the bridge structure where a shooter had set up. But that wasn't all. Another shooter had climbed one of the deck cranes and now had us pinned down in a savage crossfire.

"What now?" Knocker asked me as the incoming fire grew heavier.

I looked over at him. "I thought you might have an idea."

"Me? The only ideas I have are the crazy kind. You know, hold my beer and that shit."

He was right. I fired at the shooter on the crane and ducked back down.

I said, "Ghost Three, we need a plan. We're pinned down and running out of time."

"Give me a moment."

We kept taking fire and returning it. Our ammunition was getting low and the countdown clock even lower. Knocker called over his shoulder, "If he doesn't do something, we're going to be the next assholes in space."

"Three, what are you doing?"

"On my way, One."

That was when the van burst through the fence and onto the dock, chain-link mesh falling in its wake.

CHAPTER 2

"HERE COMES THE CAVALRY," KNOCKER SAID AS HE RELOADED. "A couple of bullets and it'll fucking fall apart."

I said, "Come on, before he gets our ride killed."

I emptied half a magazine toward the shooter in the crane and started running across the deck toward the gangplank. Knocker was close behind me, and so were the incoming bullets. Over my comms came Chambers's voice. "You two coming anytime soon?"

Looking up, I saw the van speed past the gangplank. "What the hell are you doing?"

"Moving target."

"Christ on a crutch," Knocker said.

The guard at the base of the gangplank stopped firing at the van and turned to face us. I hit him with a clenched fist, knocking him on his ass. Behind me, Knocker drew his handgun and shot him as he went past.

We hit the dock and took cover behind some crates. Bullets chewed furrows in the wood as they ricocheted into the night. I looked for the van and saw it coming back. "You guys ready?" Chambers asked.

"When this is over, I'm going to shoot the prick, Reaper, I really am," Knocker growled.

We ran from cover across the path of the approaching van. Chambers slammed on the brakes, and it skidded to a stop in front of us. We were adjacent to the cargo door. Knocker ripped it open, and we both jumped in. Incoming rounds hammered the outer skin like a summer hailstorm, except some of the hail was punching through to the interior. I slammed the door. "Go! Go!"

Chambers floored the gas pedal again and the van groaned like an old man as it tiredly started forward. The van began to pick up speed and it bounced as it hit some potholes. Up ahead, the gates to the dock were locked and there were two guards standing in front of them. They brought up their weapons and began firing.

"Hang on!" Chambers called back as we crashed through the gates.

I looked over at Knocker. "How much time—"

BOOM!

When the timer counted down, the planted explosives' blast rocked the ship, blowing containers overboard and toppling one of the three deck cranes. However, it was the secondary explosion that broke the ship's back and devastated the dock. Buildings were flattened and stored shipping containers were cast aside, swatted by a giant unseen hand. The immediate atmosphere turned orange from the large mushroom blast cloud that rose into the night sky.

"I thought operations like this were meant to be discreet. Do you realize how much damage was caused by that blast?" German asked.

"I don't think they'll welcome us back to Karachi for a while," Knocker replied.

"Must you always be so flippant?" Christine Ryan admonished him.

He glanced at me and said, "Reaper, why do people always use big words a man has trouble understanding?"

"It means disrespectful," I replied.

"Oh, shit, why didn't she just say that?"

"But that wasn't the end of it, was it?" German asked.

Holly shook her head. "These people were quite resourceful."

The blast wave buffeted the van as we drove away, causing it to almost run off the road. We started to relax because we thought we'd gotten away. However, the Russians had other ideas. We were driving away from the port and things went even further south.

"Hey, guys, we've got a problem."

I moved toward the front of the van. I said, "What?"

"Up ahead."

At first, I didn't see it. The street we were on was empty. But I was looking in the wrong area. I was looking into the darkness beyond the orange streetlamps. I should have been looking up above the horizon at the red flashing light coming toward us. It was too late when I eventually did.

"Helicopter!"

Chambers swung hard on the wheel as the asphalt in front of us erupted like mini volcanoes as rounds from the 30 mm Shipunov 2A42 canon on the helicopter slammed into it.

The rounds passed us on the left as we bounced through a shallow ditch into a vacant lot. I heard Knocker shout, "Fucking bollocks."

My head connected with the roof as we hit another bump. My neck seemed to concertina against the impact I hit that hard. Meanwhile, Chambers tried his best to keep the van on all four wheels.

It was a Mil Mi-28NM Havoc, Russian-made attack helicopter, and at that time, it was in a tight banking turn as it readied itself to make another run.

The van bounced wildly over the rough terrain as

Chambers tried to get it back in the street. Suddenly a fence appeared in front of us, and I heard him curse and charge straight at it.

The van plowed through and emerged onto a sealed driveway. He swung right as a large propane tank sprouted in the headlamps in front of us. Suddenly we were surrounded by pipes, scaffold, and all kinds of other equipment. Ahead of us sat a large tanker truck. Chambers swung around it, and just as he did, the cannon on the helicopter fired again.

The 30mm armor-piercing rounds missed us and punched into the tanker, making it explode like a bomb. The van lifted onto two wheels from the blast and slammed back down. It was about this time I realized we were in some kind of refinery.

"We need to get out of here, Ben," I shouted at him. "There're too many things in here that blow up."

"Ghost One, I need a sitrep, over," Holly called over our comms.

"We have a little problem, Bravo One."

"I'm showing you in a large refinery. Please tell me that isn't so."

"Okay, it isn't so."

"Shit. Was that an explosion I saw?"

"Wasn't us, it was the Russian helicopter."

"Lord, have mercy."

"There is good news," I said as more canon rounds smashed into the concrete apron beside us. "We're still alive."

Chambers swung right and drove under an elevated gantry past two huge oil tanks. He then swerved back the other way and into the open doorway of a large warehouse. Luckily it was empty, and through the illumination cast by the headlights, we could see that the other end was open. However, he killed the headlamps and hit the brakes.

We sat there, listening for the helicopter. My heart beat loudly in my chest as the adrenaline coursed through my veins. "I think we lost them, Reaper," Knocker said.

I let out a long, frustrated sigh. "You just had to fuck everything up."

He gave me an indignant look. "What did—"

Suddenly the helicopter was there ahead of us, framed by the large open doorway. At first it was side on, then it turned to aim its canon right at us.

"Bloody hell, this is just bonkers," Knocker growled.

"Back up!" I exclaimed at Chambers. "Back the hell up."

He slammed the gearshift into reverse and the van shot backward just as the helicopter opened fire once more. Canon rounds and tracers shot past us, one skipped off the van's roof. The motor roared as the vehicle we were in strained to go faster, as if it knew the helicopter was there to kill it.

As soon as the rear of the van was outside, Chambers swung around to the right. On our left, I could see more fires, which had been started by the most recent gunfire. Something exploded, and I thought I saw a large drum shoot skyward.

Chambers was about to move forward again when I said, "Screw it. Let me out."

I climbed from the van, followed by Knocker. Looking around, I noticed a pair of large tanks with stairs spiraling around the outside. "Follow me."

"On your six."

We ran to the stairs and started to climb. I said, "Chambers, when I tell you, bring the helicopter back this way."

"If I'm still bloody alive."

We continued climbing until we reached the top and ran along the gantry to the part that overlooked where the van would pass. I started to reload. "All right, Chambers, bring the bastard back. Knocker, full magazine."

From where we were, we could see the helicopter as it made numerous attacks on the van. Somehow though, the beat-up vehicle managed to survive the onslaught. Then it appeared around the corner of a warehouse. The helicopter followed.

I brought up the 433 and flicked the fire selector to full auto. We waited. Below us, the van roared past, and I could see in the firelight that it had a few more holes than it had before.

Then the helicopter was there, its rotors beating the air with solid slaps.

"Now, Knocker."

We opened fire at the Russian Havoc. I could see the 5.56 rounds slamming home, peppering the exterior of it. My magazine ran dry, but Knocker managed a few more shots before his ran out too. I muttered a curse as I watched the helicopter fly on, oblivious to the bee stings inflicted upon it.

Then it seemed to falter, hesitated in its forward motion. Then, from nowhere, it fell from the sky, hitting the concrete apron and exploding into a fireball.

"Top stuff, Reaper," Knocker said to me.

"Yeah, now we need to get out of here before the Karachi police lock us all in a deep dark hole."

We ran back down the stairs and found Chambers waiting for us. Climbing into the van, we found a large hole in the side. Knocker said, "Good for those hot days."

"You blokes are bloody nuts," Chambers growled as he floored the gas pedal.

"I'd like to say it keeps us alive," I replied. "But I won't."

I slammed the door of the van and walked toward Holly. "It's them. It damn well has to be."

"We don't know that, John."

"Bullshit, boss," Knocker growled. "We have a shipload of weapons, Russians watching over it, and a damn Russian helicopter comes out of nowhere."

"If you're right, where were the weapons going?"

Knocker reached into his shirt and took out the papers he'd grabbed from the bridge. "They were headed for the DRC."

Holly looked thoughtful. "If this is true, and I'm not saying it isn't, it would mean that the Russians are supporting the rebels."

"Anything to piss off the west," Knocker said.

"But what is their reason, their end game?"

"I don't like the sound of that, Reaper."

I nodded. "It sounds ominous, don't it?"

"It'll have to wait. Let's get packed up. Time to go home."

"Roger that."

Julia Firth came over to us, a wry smile on her face. "You guys are badass."

"Sometimes we're just bad," I replied.

"I'm thinking we need to get a beer when we get back to London."

Still pumped up on adrenaline, I smiled. "I think maybe we should."

Word had filtered back to Moscow about the Karachi incident. I say filtered, it actually hit like a sledgehammer. We realized this because of the reaction it got. Four of the Gods met dressed in their usual attire. The uniforms of the old USSR. At the head of the table, Mikhail Shatov looked less than impressed. "We are here because of Karachi. Someone tell me about what happened."

An officer to his right said, "To keep it in basic terms,

Comrade, the shipment was blown up. Somehow, word leaked about it, and it was attacked."

"Yes, but by whom?" Shatov snarled as he slapped his hand down on the table.

The same officer opened a file and extracted four pieces of paper and he slid them in front of their commander. "Our intelligence people gathered these."

The general looked down and stared at the pictures before him. "It is them, again. How is it that they seem to appear right at the most inopportune time?"

"We think that maybe they never knew it was us. They just acted on the intelligence they received."

Shatov thought for a moment. "Maybe we can throw them off or kill them. Put together a team. They must be expendable."

"I'm sure I can gather one."

Shatov slid a picture across the table and said, "This person will be their target."

"Yes, sir."

"Nothing about this team can lead back to us. In fact, I want it to lead somewhere else. Do you understand?"

"I think so."

"Good. Make it so. I will talk to the President."

CHAPTER 3

THEY CAME FOR US IN LONDON. BY US, I MEAN FOR THEIR target. Luke Chapman and Ben Chambers were out together at a pub in London's East End. They'd spent the evening there watching a rugby match, and now they were leaving. Chapman slapped his friend on the shoulder after they emerged and said, "I'll see you for the debrief tomorrow."

Chambers said that they went their different ways after that. From what we could gather, scrolling through security footage, street cameras, and anything else we could find, they picked up Chapman a block from the pub. Four men in a dark cargo van. They were professionals, and the kidnapping was over within thirty seconds.

They kept him for twenty-four hours. Twenty-four hours of torture and pain. When they were finished with him, they dumped his body in the most public place possible. Outside Buckingham Palace.

And while London dealt with the horror of it all, we worked the problem.

"The body outside Buckingham Palace was one of your people?" Christine Ryan asked, perplexed.

Holly nodded. "Yes, ma'am."

"Why wasn't that in the report?"

"We are—were a covert team. We don't put everything in writing. Just the stuff we think you need to know. Our team was expendable."

"Does this happen often?"

"All the time."

We finally tracked the killers to a derelict housing estate in West London. It was a lot like Heygate Estate was in South London years ago. Knocker and I went in while Holly, Lynda, and Chambers were set up in a cargo van off-site.

We'd combed through intel for twenty-four hours until we found them. Four men, associates of the Russian Mafia.

"What the hell is the Russian Mafia doing targeting one of our people?" Knocker asked when we found out.

I had shaken my head. "It doesn't make sense, does it?"

"Not by a long sight."

"This branch is known for arms trafficking," Holly told us.

"Are you saying that this could be revenge for the operation in Karachi?" I asked.

"It looks that way."

"What about our other friends?" Knocker asked.

"They've gone quiet. Left all the speaking to their new president."

And Sergey Lash had been making quite a noise. One of the first things he'd done was start trading openly with North Korea, followed by Iran. With an election coming up in the UK, both men vying for the top job had condemned the new Russian leader in the hope of buying votes. However, the front runner was the new man on the block. A candidate much younger than his opponent and who was picking up much of the younger vote.

But I digress. We were hunting killers, and that is what brought us to the housing estate.

Knocker and I were wearing all our normal kit. Jeans, shirts, body armor. It was the middle of the day, so we didn't need our NVGs.

The estate consisted of one large building of ten floors surrounded by five smaller ones of six floors. There was even a small shopping center on-site at the base of the main tower.

Intel had the ones we were after in the main tower. Somewhere on the third or fourth floor. We weren't sure where. The other thing we had to watch for was homeless people. The towers were a major hangout for them.

As we approached the main building, we entered through a chainmesh fence gate. The lock had been cut and the chain left hanging. I said, "Bravo One, it looks like the lock on the main gate has been cut recently."

"Copy, Ghost One. Watch your six."

We hurried across the open area toward the main doors, which would let us into the primary tower. Our suppressed 433s were up as we swept left and right, looking for targets.

The doors were smashed open. It wasn't recent, they'd been like that for a long time. The dirt and rubbish on the tiled floor were scattered everywhere. Either side of us were stores. All were glass-fronted. Some were broken, others were not. All were vacant except for shelving.

We moved past a bank of elevators, each was taped off as a warning. When we reached the stairwell, Knocker decided he wanted to take point. We started up, arriving at the first landing. Knocker covered the stairs while I opened the door and looked inside to make sure it was clear.

On the other side of the door looked to be a large dining hall. I said, "Bravo One, why the hell would an apartment block have a large dining hall?"

"When it was built, it was believed it would bring residents together as a community. The thing was, before anyone could move in, the owners went broke, and the complex lay dormant. Now, in a few months, it looks like the demolition crews will be moving in."

I pulled back out and touched Knocker on the shoulder. He started up the stairs again toward the next level. Again, once we reached the landing, he watched the stairwell while I opened the door, looking for any surprises.

"Bravo One, second floor looks good."

"Ghost One, we're picking up some movement on three. Advise caution."

"Copy that."

When we reached the third floor, I opened the door and peered down the hallway, which looked clear. With Knocker behind me, we started forward. In my ear, Holly said, "X-Rays possibly in the third apartment on your right."

We made it to the second apartment before they got nervous and sprang their trap early. A fragmentation grenade bounced into the hallway and rolled to a stop. I felt my eyes widen as I realized what it was.

"Grenade!"

"Not again," Knocker growled as he threw himself flat.

The explosion washed along the hallway toward us, the heat intense. Dirt and debris rained down from above and I could taste the grit in my mouth. My ears rang, and somewhere in the distance, I could hear automatic weapons firing.

Except it wasn't in the distance, it was along the hallway. I rolled onto my back to free my 433. Instead of rolling again, I just brought it up and opened fire.

Someone cried out in pain after a 5.56 round found flesh. Moments later, Knocker joined the party, and we laid down some good suppressing fire.

I glanced left, and I noticed a door to the apartment opposite had blown open. The last thing I wanted to do was get trapped inside an apartment, but the hallway was worse. "Follow me."

Moments later, I dived through the open doorway, followed by Knocker.

Sucking in deep breaths, I said, "Bravo One, we're taking heavy fire. I say again, we're taking heavy fire."

"Roger that, we saw the explosion. Are you alright?"

Knocker was using the doorway for cover while firing and cursing the ambushers. "So far, we're still in the fight."

"Hold on to your hats, gents," Chambers said. "Looks like we've got more X-Rays inbound."

"It was a fucking trap," I growled.

"I'm counting six more heavily armed guys on their way up."

"Sounds like a good day," I replied and reloaded my 433. "Ghost One out."

———

After I had signed off, Chambers looked at Holly and said, "We need to go in there."

She had shaken her head. "No, we wait."

"They're outnumbered."

"That's where they live."

———

"Knocker, are you good?"

"Having a fucking great time, Reaper."

"We've got more X-Rays on the way up."

He fired a burst and pulled back. "I hope they bring beer."

I rushed to the other side of the apartment, where a sliding glass door led out onto a balcony. It was locked and jammed. I didn't have time to screw around so I shot it and the glass shattered, raining onto the carpet and tiled balcony floor.

Stepping through the glass to the balcony, I looked around. The rails for each unit on the same level were close together, the ones below I figured we could reach. I had a plan and poked my head back in and said, "Hey, can you hold?"

"For how long?" Knocker shouted back.

"That long."

"Just don't forget about me."

"Give me a few minutes and I'll be back."

He started firing again in short bursts. Meanwhile, I climbed out over the balcony rail with the ambition of getting down to the next. I tested the top one before I went. It wasn't the best, but seemed stable enough. It should have been easy, but years of neglect made the journey precarious. Especially when the rail tore away from its mounts.

I fell straight down. Plummeted was probably a better word. I grabbed the rail of the second floor as I went past. And true to form, it gave way too and my journey continued.

As I fell, I made one last desperate attempt to arrest my fall. My hands locked onto a first-floor rail, and I jerked to a stop.

Pain shot through my shoulders with the sudden stop. A moan escaped my lips, and for a moment, I just hung there. I could hear the gunfire from above. It seemed to have intensified.

"Knocker, what's going on?"

"Their friends just got here."

"Which end of the hallway?"

"The way we came in."

"Okay," I grunted as I hauled myself up over the rail. "Hang in there, I'm on my way."

"Where are you?"

"First floor."

"What—no, forget it. I don't want to know."

I had to shoot my way into the apartment so I could traverse it. As I did so, a voice said, "Hey, man, what the fuck are you doing?"

A guy stepped in front of me. He was armed with what looked like a machete. He held it up threateningly. It was then he finally noticed my weapon. Suddenly he couldn't back up quick enough. "Hey, man, take what you want."

"Just get the hell out of my way, pal."

He stepped aside and I hurried to the door. I opened it and jogged along the hallway toward the stairwell. Then as I had done not long ago, I started up them to the third floor.

"Reaper, I'm on my last mag. If you have a plan, now would be a good time to put it into action."

"Just hold on," I said into my comms.

I passed the second landing, and as I continued up, I saw the shooter at the door on the third-floor landing.

My 433 came up and my finger stroked the trigger twice. Even though the weapon was suppressed, it was still loud in the stairwell. The shooter at the door slumped forward across the threshold.

Leaning against the doorjamb, I peered along the hallway. Easing back, I muttered into my comms, "Don't fire to your right."

"Copy that."

"On three, I need you to cover left."

"Ready when you are."

Deep breath, then, "Three."

Breaking cover, I started along the hallway. Knocker appeared and covered left as I asked him to. As I reached the first open door, a shooter appeared. I shot him and then another in the doorway opposite.

Moving through the doorway, I found another shooter

taking cover just inside. He died next. Two bullets in the head.

Opposite, where I'd shot the second shooter, another appeared, but this time he was aware of my presence. I threw myself sideways out of his firing line. My shoulder hit the floor and pain jarred through my body.

Bullets hammered into the walls, making clouds of debris erupt from them as they took on a life of their own. I rolled away and came to my feet. The shooter across the hallway threw caution to the wind and came after me.

Like his friends, he died for his impatience.

The shooting stopped. I peeked around the jamb and saw two shooters retreating toward the other end of the hallway. They never made it, dying with the last four rounds from Knocker's 433 in their backs.

I stepped out into the hallway. "Hey, Eddie Charlton, are you all right?"

Knocker stepped out into the hallway. "What's this Eddie Charlton shit?"

"He's the only guy I could think of."

"You know he was a snooker player, right?"

"I knew he was something. Let's check these guys out."

We gave the bodies the once over and found all of them had some kind of mafia tattoos on them. But they were different. We'd fought enough of them over the years to know that they should have been the same. Then we saw why.

"Prison tattoos," Knocker said.

"Yes. This was a setup."

"Ghost One, we're picking up inbound police. You should leave."

"On our way. Out."

"You just left the mess for the Metropolitan Police to clean up?" German asked.

"*Sometimes the best choice is to ask for forgiveness later,*" Holly said.

"*Except if you end up before some bullshit board that are out for blood because people did their job,*" Knocker growled.

"*If you did your job properly, there wouldn't be a mess,*" Christine Ryan said huffily.

"*If we did our job your way, this country would have ceased to exist a long time ago. Well before this.*"

"*Don't be so absurd.*"

"*What the hell would you know about the world of Black Ops? You sit in your ivory fucking tower drinking gin and tonic and think everything is bloody perfect.*"

I grabbed Knocker by the arm. He took a deep breath and relaxed a little.

Christine Ryan's eyes narrowed. "*Have you finished, Mr. Jensen?*"

"*I suppose so.*"

"*I will have you know that I haven't always been a politician. I was once Miss Smith.*"

Knocker stared hard at her. "*That's right, Mr. Jensen. I have been there and done that as they say. I worked in Moscow, Germany, Afghanistan, and South America. So, yes, Mr. Jensen, I do know about the world of Black Ops.*"

He continued staring at her but remained silent. Then she said, "*Please continue.*"

When we returned, we went to the debriefing room to discuss what we had found. Brian Short joined us as we worked through it. "They weren't Russian Mafia as we know it," I said.

"What do you mean?" Short asked.

"They were like a slapped-together crew out of prison."

"For what reason?"

"To come after us, I guess. To make us look the other way," I suggested.

"Away from what?"

"I don't know."

"Follow it. Look into whatever it takes to get an outcome."

"I have a contact here in London who might be able to shed some light," Holly said.

Short nodded. "Go, talk to them. But before you go, is there anything out of the DRC or the arms shipment?"

"Nothing apart from the theory about Russian Mafia shipping them."

"Which is a shit theory," Knocker said.

Short's gaze hardened. "Prove it then. Find me something that says it is."

"Yes, sir," Holly said. "John, you come with me."

I nodded. "Lead the way."

_____

She took me to a theater in London's East End. It was the middle of the day by now, and as she found a park, I said, "Holly, are you sure he will be here?"

"He's always here," she replied. "He has something about rehearsals."

We climbed out of the SUV and went inside. A Glock 19 was tucked in the back of my pants, pressing against my spine. We were here to see Willy Harris, king of the London Underground. If anyone knew anything, Holly claimed it would be Willy.

Inside was dark. Not pitch black, but dark enough. The sound of voices reached out to us, and when we entered the main theater, I could see why. On stage were four people rehearsing lines.

Holly stopped and looked around. Then she looked up behind us and said, "Up one."

We returned to the foyer, locating the staircase to the gallery. We then followed the narrow hallway around, past the private boxes, to the entrance to the balcony seating area. When we entered, both of us were greeted by a big guy wearing a suit and trying to act menacing. Holly said, "We're here to see your boss."

"Wait here," he grunted and turned away.

I watched him closely as he walked along the aisle. "Who is this guy again?"

"Willy?"

"Yeah."

"He runs the London Underground. He's like the crime boss's crime boss."

"How is it that someone hasn't put him out of business?" I asked.

"We need someone to control what happens on the street. He's MI5s asset. They look the other way on the proviso that he feeds them intel. He has no such deal with the Met."

The doorman had a word with his boss and then came back to us, laboring up the sloped floor. "He says go away."

"Tell him that if he doesn't want to talk right now, I'll wait."

He rolled his eyes and walked back down. Once more he talked to his boss, and Willy glared back over his shoulder, throwing his hands into the air in a frustrated gesture. Then his man started back up toward us. It was then I saw a woman sit up from where she had her face buried in the mobster's crotch.

"Someone will not be happy," I said.

"Must be his latest whatever you want to call her."

"I can think of a few things," I replied.

"The boss will see you," the bodyguard panted.

I slapped him on the shoulder. "Stay up here, buddy. You look like you could use the rest."

We walked down and stopped near Willy. He gave us a

look of disdain. "Interrupt a man when he's being entertained."

Holly looked at the woman beside him. Her lipstick was smudged, no doubt the excess was somewhere currently unseen. Holly said, "You can get back to it when we're done, Willy."

"We're done now. Go away."

Holly looked at the woman. "Go fix your lipstick while we talk."

She glanced at Willy, and he nodded. Getting to her feet she disappeared back up the aisle. The mobster looked at us. "Okay, Holly, you have my attention. What do you want?"

"There were some new people in London. Supposedly Russian Mafia. They would have come in over the past couple of days."

"Russians you say?"

"Yes."

"I might have heard something about it."

I stared at him. He glared back, taking an instant dislike to the way I was looking at him. "What the fuck are you looking at?"

I shrugged.

He looked at Holly. "Tell your friend to go away. I don't like him."

"Just stick with the task at hand, Willy."

"What do I get out of it, Holly?"

"My sincerest gratitude, Willy," she replied.

"Maybe you could hang around after we're done. I'll tell Jackie to go home, and you can finish what she started."

Right then I wanted to throttle the guy. However, I'd underestimated Holly, who stepped forward seductively and ran her hand along the mobster's thigh until it reached his crotch. His eyes lit up, but it lasted all of a heartbeat as she closed her grip hard. Willy's eyes bulged and his face went from red to a deeper shade of purple. Holly leaned in close and said, "If you ever suggest something like that again, I'll squeeze your balls even harder so that they pop under the pressure. Besides, the only dicks I suck are the ones that will get me higher up the ladder."

She released her grip, and he groaned in relief. Coughing, he gasped and took a minute or so to regain his composure. "Fine."

"Now, tell us about the Russians."

"The ones you killed over at the complex?"

"They're the ones."

"I was asked to provide accommodations for a specialist team. No questions. The money was good, so I made the deal."

"Who came to you?"

He shrugged. "I don't know. It was done through a third party. All I had to do was provide them with a place to stay and transport."

I took a step forward and grabbed his shirt. "You got our friend fucking killed."

"I didn't know they were here for you. I was told nothing."

I let him go.

"You know where from, don't you?" Holly asked him.

"Yes, Russia. I told you that. You already fucking knew it."

"Holly shook her head. Not what I mean. Where did they come from?"

"It looked like out of the penal system. I heard them talking. They were discussing what prisons they were in."

"So, they weren't mafia."

"No. They were just hired to do a job."

"Who by?" Holly asked.

"They didn't say."

I heard voices and glanced up to where the bodyguard was standing. He was talking to two men and looked at us then back at the newcomers. What happened next seemed to happen in slow motion.

One of the men reached under their coat and pulled a handgun. Within a couple of heartbeats, he'd shot the bodyguard in the chest.

Two shots.

Close range.

"BANG! BANG!

"Gun!" I shouted and launched myself at Holly. We ended up on the floor together between a row of seats just as the second shooter opened fire.

I heard the bullets hit flesh, the sound is unmistakable. Willy grunted and collapsed sideways in his seat. I grabbed my Glock and came up off the floor. There was no one there. The shooters had disappeared.

"They've gone," I said to Holly and started running toward the balcony's exit. By the time I got into the hallway, they were well and truly out of there.

I went back to where Holly was crouched over Willy. "He's gone."

"Someone tidying up loose ends."

Holly straightened up. "Let's get out of here, I don't feel like answering questions."

We exited the theater and climbed back into the SUV. The first of the police cars was just pulling up as we left the area.

"Where are we going?" I asked her.

"I need a beer."

We drove for a while before finding a pub, parking, entering the bar, and ordering beers. Holly's cell rang numerous times, and she rejected each call. I said, "You know he's getting pissed off every time you do that."

"He'll get over it," she replied. "Sometimes small doses of Short are all I can take."

We chose to sit in a far corner of the pub out of sight but

where we could see the door. I could also see the television from our position, and as the bar person flicked through the channels, he stopped on the BBC news station.

I frowned as I watched it. Not sure what I was seeing at first, then it clicked, and I suddenly knew. "Holly, we need to go to the DRC."

She turned and looked. Sergey Lash was talking to the Russian media, announcing they were sending advisers into the DRC to support the rebels against a corrupt regime.

"They'll be there," I said to her. "This has their names written all over it."

Holly nodded in resignation. "We'd better have a chat with Brian."

CHAPTER 4

"You can't be serious," Short stated. "You want to pack your team up and send them into a potential war zone?"

"The French have peacekeepers on the ground, Brian."

"And look at what they're doing. Fuck all." He looked at me. "Well, what do you have to say?"

"I'm telling you, whatever is going on in the DRC, the Gods are involved."

"Why? Why does it have to be them? Couldn't it be just a shitty rebellion in a shitty country?"

Holly nodded at Lynda who put a folder on Short's desk. "What is this?"

He opened it and Holly said, "My people were originally looking into the DRC. Last week, a UN aid convoy disappeared in the circled part of the region. Not far from there is a diamond mine. No one has had any contact with it for the past ten days. The company who owns it believes that it may have fallen into the hands of the rebels."

"So?"

"Have a look at the second and third photos."

Short took it out. "Where is this?"

"The first is a satellite photo from three weeks ago.

Everything looks fine. The second is from ten days ago. Take a look at the vehicles."

Short leaned closer, and I saw his expression change. "Russian trucks, and it looks like armed men."

"Exactly. Lash is announcing advisers headed to the DRC today. Someone has been in the country for the past two weeks. Now, I have one more photo for you to look at."

Short took it. His silence lasted a while before he said, "Who is he?"

"We don't know. We tried facial rec and got nothing. We ran everything we could find. There is no record of him entering the country or him leaving. For all we know, he could still be there. It's like someone has gone to the trouble of erasing everything about him. You can tell by the uniform he's Russian."

"There is something about the uniform."

"It's old-style Soviet Union."

"And you say there is nothing anywhere about him that you can find?"

"Yes, sir. The man is a ghost."

Short sighed. "All right, you've got me. You and your two specialists are all I'll clear. No one else."

"I need my team, sir."

He shook his head. "No, take what you can get, Holly, and call it a victory. I'll let the resident team there know you're on your way."

"Yes, sir."

"Oh, one more thing, don't get yourself killed."

"Yes, sir."

———

Kinshasa was hot, humid, and almost soul-destroying. There were fires throughout the city. The result of bomb blasts from an embedded fifth column inside the limits.

There were numerous civilians remaining in the city, but a lot had moved on as well.

Going in using the cover of reporters, we each wore a visible flak jacket with press written on it but also had Glocks hidden on our person. A hotel in the city was the safehouse, cover being good because all the press used it.

The team leader was a redheaded guy named Barry Foster. He'd been in the country for twelve months as the senior man on station.

At four p.m. the day we arrived, we were down in the bar drinking beer with the other reporters and written press. "Where are you from, Kane?" a guy named Fuller asked. He was from a Canadian paper.

"Manchester Herald," I replied. "Just started and they sent me here."

"An American?"

"Sure. Got sick of life across the Atlantic."

"What about your friends?"

I sipped my beer. "Ray is my photographer and Miss Smith is a freelancer. We're traveling together."

"You could have picked a better place," an Australian newsman said. "Now that the Russians are officially here, the shit will really hit the fan."

"What do you mean officially?" Holly asked.

"They've been here for around three weeks."

"How do you know that?" I asked.

"We get around and see things. I went and interviewed a rebel commander about that time, and he let it slip. We've been getting reports about them as well from the civilians."

I nodded. "What happened to the aid convoy?"

"They're fucked," a new voice joined the conversation.

"Who are you?"

"Kyle Lincoln, Atlanta Tribune."

"Care to elaborate?"

"Jungle drums. They're rarely wrong."

I glanced at Holly who was staring at me over her beer as she drank. "Has anyone been out there to verify it?"

They all looked at each other. It was the Australian who said, "Nah, mate. We don't leave the city."

"The only people outside the city are the guys fighting," Lincoln said.

WHOOMP!

The hotel seemed to shake. The Australian said, "Another bomb."

"Do you get many?" Holly asked.

"Three, four a day at the moment."

"Is there anyone who will guide me out of the city?" I asked.

They all looked at me as though I was crazy. Lincoln said, "You don't want to do that, pal."

"If I'm to get a story, it might be a good way to get it."

"A good way to get killed. There have been three journos killed already in this conflict."

"What about the mine nobody has heard from?"

"Don't tell me, you want to look at that as well," said Fuller.

"Can't hurt."

The Australian shook his head. He raised his beer and said, "Gentlemen, I propose a toast. To the craziest mother-fucker here, may he get to live for twenty-four hours before some bastard kills him."

We finished our beers and went upstairs into the suite where the MI6 crew hung out. As soon as we entered the room, Foster turned and said, "You really want to head up to where that aid convoy disappeared?"

"Yes."

"The French have started to construct a compound up that way to protect the aid convoys. I might be able to get you up there. Find a guide when you get there."

"That would be great, thanks."

"Are you sure we should be going up there alone, Reaper?" Knocker asked.

"Not us, me."

"The fuck you say."

"You and Holly see what you can dig up around here. I'll be fine."

Knocker looked skeptically at Holly. She shrugged. "I know, but someone has to go."

"I still think it's a fucked up idea."

———

Meanwhile, as we were making plans, others were doing the same thing. Lazar Noskov was meeting with Edo Wissa in a small village a hundred kilometers from the capital. "I will give you some of my men to help," Noskov said.

"My friend, you already have control of one diamond mine. Why do you want another?"

"If we control that mine as well, then we control a good proportion of the country's wealth. Once it is taken, I will have soldiers placed there to ensure that production will continue."

"And what will happen when the war is over?"

"Like the other mine, you will control both."

What Noskov wasn't saying was that while the fighting continued, he and his men were siphoning off hundreds of millions of dollars in ice to send back to Moscow.

"What about the French peacekeepers and their base?"

"They don't belong there. We can make them go away."

"You mean attack them," Wissa said.

"Do you want your country or not?" Noskov asked. "If you lose this fight, General, the west will control it forever."

"I will see what happens."

"Never mind, General. Russia will stand with you."

"Only because Russia wants our wealth. I am beginning

to think that Russia is no better than the west. Maybe I should reconsider once everything has come to fruition."

Noskov could feel his anger rising within. He glanced at the other man in the room. The general's bodyguard. The man's face had remained passive throughout. The Russian nodded. "Okay, General, if that is the way you feel."

Noskov turned and left the room, closing the door behind him. Moments later, the gunshot came. It was time to move things to the next level.

The hotel was abuzz the following morning. As I came down from the suite I ran into Holly and Foster. "What's happening?"

"The shit has hit the fan, is what," Foster said.

"How so?"

"Russian mercenaries have seized the Palais de la Nation. The president is under house arrest and the new man in charge is on his way into the city."

"Wissa?"

"No, that's where it really spins out of control. Wissa was murdered by his bodyguard yesterday. He's been replaced by a man named Simon Elia."

"Who is Elia?"

Holly shook her head. "That's just it, no one has ever heard of him. The word is that as soon as he takes office, he will order out all peacekeepers, UN aid agencies, and foreign press."

I thought for a moment. "How did Russian advisers suddenly become a force to take over the DRC Palais de la Nation?"

Holly said, "We're waiting for Lash to hold a conference in Moscow. I have a feeling I know what is coming."

I nodded. "Protectorate."

"Uh-huh."

"Are they mobilizing forces?" I asked.

"Not enough."

"Then maybe the protectorate thing is a step too far. As it is, when Elia takes over, he'll have over one hundred thousand troops on the ground as a start. If he goes with conscription, he could get double that."

"I guess we'll have to wait and see."

Looking at Foster, I asked, "Did you get me some transport?"

"You're still going?" he asked incredulously.

I nodded. "The concentration of Russian advisers is in that area. Apart from those that are now in Kinshasa. I want to know what they're doing up there."

"Fine. Be ready in an hour."

He left us and I looked around at the press people who were running around like headless chickens, trying to get a story over the phone. Holly said, "Are you sure you want to go, John?"

"Like I said, they're up to something and we need to find out."

Lincoln stopped near us. "Are you coming?"

"Where?"

"To the Palais de la Nation. There's going to be a speech when Elia arrives."

I looked at Holly. "You go and take Knocker with you."

"Are you sure?"

"Yeah, it'll be fine."

———

An hour later, I met Foster in the foyer. He ushered me out to an SUV, and we left the city. Waiting for me was a British Chinook.

Foster said, "They will take you to the French base

where they will help you out. Weapons, things like that. Don't get yourself killed."

I nodded. "Thanks."

When I climbed aboard, I was greeted by the loadmaster. "Welcome aboard. Strap yourself in and we'll be leaving directly."

"I didn't think there were any British forces in the DRC?"

The loadmaster smiled at me. "I'm not British, I'm Irish."

"Fair enough."

As soon as I was strapped in, the ramp was up, and the helicopter lifted into the sky. It flew low over the terrain to start with before gaining more height. I was on my way, but to what, I had no idea.

"Mr. Kane, what did you hope to achieve going off on your own?" German asked.

"Just as I said before. Something was happening and we needed to know what. Looking back on what we know now, I think it was the right thing to do."

He looked at Holly. "And you supported this...madness?"

"I thought it was crazy. But if we wanted to know what was happening, it was something that needed to be done."

German sighed and shuffled through some of the papers in front of him. "Fine, let's have a look at Miss Smith and Mr. Jensen. It would seem that they walked into some kind of storm."

CHAPTER 5

THE PALAIS DE LA NATION WAS HUGE. WHEN KNOCKER AND Holly pulled up, there were troops everywhere. A mix of DRC and Russian. Flags of both countries were flying, and a large crowd was gathering. Some of the citizens were even armed.

"What do you make of it?" Holly asked Knocker.

"I hate coups. I've been mixed up in them before. None of it ends well. Especially for the civilian population."

The press contingent was gathered at the front of the crowd. It was being held back by a row of armed DRC soldiers. A podium had been set up on the greenest part of the lawn and a red carpet ran up to the stairs to be utilized by the new president.

Knocker swatted at a fly and muttered something illegible. He pretended to examine his camera while continually looking around the crowd and guards. "Do you figure these Russians were the ones responsible for the coup?"

Holly nodded. "Most probably."

Suddenly, the press crowd started to move. Knocker looked to his right and saw the small cavalcade driving in. A limousine broke away from the procession and crossed the lawn close to the podium. Moments after it stopped, three Russian bodyguards climbed out. The third of them opened the back door. And Simon Elia alighted.

Knocker figured the new president to be in his early forties. Dressed in a suit and unshaven, he looked around as though lost. A hand from one of his bodyguards guided him to the podium.

While everybody's attention was turned to his movements, Knocker noticed the last man to climb from the limousine. He was a white man dressed in a suit. Knocker figured he was somewhere in his late sixties or early seventies.

"Holly, get a look at this."

She turned her attention to the man and stared at him. He must have sensed her gaze because he turned his head and stared straight at them. "He has to be a Russian."

Knocker nodded. "I'll see if I can get a photo of him."

Raising the camera, he took a photo, pulling it back down quickly and letting it hang by its strap. Meanwhile, Elia had moved to the podium. He stood there listening to the cheers, posing for photos. Holly said, "They all act like it's a good thing."

"I'm guessing most of these people are rebels," Knocker said.

Eventually, the crowd quieted down enough for Elia to begin his speech. "Friends and countrymen, what a great day for the Democratic Republic of the Congo. There are so many people I would like to thank, including our friends from halfway across the world in Russia. Without their support, none of this would have been possible."

Elia nodded to the man in the suit and said, "So thank you for all you have done, my friend."

The Russian looked uncomfortable about having the attention drawn to him. It was obvious that Elia had just gone off script. The man wanted to remain in the shadows. "That was a fuck-up," Knocker said.

"What do you mean?" asked Holly, glancing at Knocker.

"The look our Russian friend just gave the new president was one of death."

"You know what that means?"

"Yes. There's a good chance he's one of them."

Suddenly, two big Russians appeared beside them. One, a big man about six foot four, looked at Knocker and said, "I want your camera."

Knocker stared at him and said, "Be fucked, you do. I work for the press, mate. You know, freedom of speech and all that shit."

"Give me the camera."

"Go…get…fucked."

The man looked unhappy about being unsuccessful, but as Knocker guessed, he didn't want to make a scene. So instead, they walked away. Holly said, "You know they aren't done."

"Yeah, I figured as much."

Meanwhile, Elia kept rambling with his speech. "My friends, today is a great day for trade. A whole new market has opened up for our great nation. Gone will be the west's dictatorship of what we can sell to them. Their taxes on our goods and the exorbitant taxes they put on theirs. And from this day, our wealth will come from our own riches. And all of us will share in those riches. I am announcing today that all of the mining operations within our borders will revert back to DRC control. All foreign companies will be given one week to be gone from our soil. All UN aid agencies and peacekeepers will be given the same time. Any armed forces on our sovereign soil after that will be declared as enemies of the DRC and dealt with accordingly."

A loud cheer erupted among the civilians.

Knocker leaned close to Holly. "Tell me, what do the Russians get out of this?"

"Diamonds."

"But why diamonds? Why do they need them?" Knocker asked.

"Well, look at what they've done so far. They've just taken control of a new oil field and now they can have a shitload of diamonds."

"But supporting a rebellion just for diamonds doesn't make sense," Knocker replied.

"Maybe you should ask our friend."

"Maybe. But I've seen enough. Let's get out of here before our friends come back."

They left it at that. The photo of the nameless man gave them a lot of unanswered questions. Climbing into their SUV, they started along the driveway and back toward their hotel.

Knocker looked into the mirror. "Shit, we've got a tail."

Before Holly could speak, her cell rang. She listened for a moment and then asked a couple of questions before hanging up. "We have somewhere else we have to be."

———

"This is a first," Knocker said. "A meeting at a landfill site. Fucking stinks."

They had lost the tail soon after leaving the press conference and getting the call. Holly had remained tight-lipped about the meeting, only telling Knocker it was an old friend who wanted to speak to her.

Ten minutes after they arrived at the landfill a black sedan approached from the opposite direction. Knocker said, "I gather this is your friend."

"Yes."

Two men got out, one younger than the other. Knocker

figured the more youthful one to be a bodyguard/driver. The other man walked toward them. Holly embraced him and he returned the gesture. They kissed on the cheek and the older man stepped back.

"Georgy, this is Raymond. Raymond, this is Georgy. My old friend from when I was a little girl. He and my father knew each other."

He gave her a quizzical look but remained silent. Holly turned back to him and said, "What are you doing here?"

"FSB chief of station."

Knocker heard the words and was immediately on guard. "What the fuck is this, Holly?"

"Just relax. Like I said, Georgy is a friend."

She saw the concern on Georgy's face and knew there was something terribly wrong. "Holly child, what I am about to tell you could get me killed."

"Then don't. Just get back in your vehicle and drive away, Georgy."

He shook his head. "I cannot. What is happening to my country is very bad and people in the right places should know."

"Know what?"

"Know what they are doing."

"Who?" Holly asked.

"The Generals," Georgy replied. "They are called The Gods of War."

Holly kept a straight face and remained calm. "Tell me about them, Georgy."

"They were started back in the Cold War days. Five generals who came up with scenarios just in case Mother Russia was ever under threat."

"Do you know their names?" Knocker asked.

Georgy shook his head. "Only a few know who they are."

"Georgy, do you know Mikhail Shatov?"

He frowned at the name. "Not for a long time. He and I served together in Afghanistan."

"And Pavel Krupin?"

He nodded. "Yes, but both are dead now. They died in a plane crash."

Holly just stared at him.

He could tell by the stare alone all he needed to know. "No, Holly? They are alive?"

"Mikhail is. Krupin died in purgatory under Mikhail's name. We figure they threatened his family."

"What do you mean?"

"We believe that Mikhail is a God of War. They massacred a village in Syria, and now we believe they are after the DRC's diamond mines."

"That makes sense. They will need—"

THWAP!

"Christ," Knocker growled as his hand went for his Glock. He looked in the direction the shot had emanated and saw Georgy's bodyguard with a suppressed handgun. He was aiming at Holly. "Holly, down!"

The bullet missed just as she moved.

Knocker fired three shots as he strode purposefully forward. Each round hit the bodyguard in the chest. The man fell to the ground and Knocker ran over to him. He found him still breathing and crouched down. "You're fucked, mate. Where did you come from? Who told you to kill him?"

The dying man grinned, showing bloodstained teeth. Then he died.

Knocker went through his pockets and found nothing useful. But then he noticed something and turned his head. The man was wearing an earwig. "Holly, check him for an earwig."

"He doesn't have one."

Knocker came to his feet. "We need to go, now."

"I-I can't just leave him."

"Unless you want to be here when his friends arrive, you've got no choice, girl. Now, move." They ran toward the SUV. "Holly, you drive."

Knocker opened the rear of the vehicle and took out a 433. He made sure it was ready to go before climbing in. Holly floored the gas pedal, and the SUV shot forward. "Obviously they didn't trust him."

"I can't believe it. He was a good man."

"Now he's a dead man—look out!"

Three sedans came out of nowhere, a man leaning out of the passenger window of the first. He had an automatic weapon in his hands and opened fire with it. Even though Holly swerved to throw his aim off, bullets still found the SUV.

"Turn right up here," Knocker said.

Holly did as she was told and accelerated faster. "You know where this goes, right?"

"Yes."

More bullets peppered the SUV, and immediately after, Holly was wrestling with the wheel. "Damn it."

"Stop here."

She trod hard on the brakes and it skidded to a stop. Knocker climbed out and sprayed the lead vehicle. He saw the windscreen go, and the sedan lurched to the right before crashing into a ditch filled with garbage and water.

"Get a weapon, move."

She reached into the back and took out the spare 433. Then she tossed Knocker his webbing and grabbed the other for herself. He said, "Follow me."

Running toward the shit ditch, he jumped across it, pausing on the other side. He waited for Holly to jump and made sure she was safely across. Then they disappeared into the slums.

"Take me back to your relationship with Georgy, Miss Smith,"

Christine Ryan said. "Would it be highly unusual for someone in your position to be friends with a Russian station chief?"

"Georgy was a good man. I would have trusted him implicitly. That was why he came to me with what he knew."

"It wasn't much though, was it? Maybe if he knew more, then we wouldn't be in this mess."

I placed my hand on Holly's arm, feeling the tension course through her.

German said, "Did anyone else know of your relationship with Georgy?"

"No."

"Have you ever given him information about national secrets?"

"Of course not."

"But he was going to do it to you."

"Which I took to mean that something bad was happening. And guess what? He was fucking right."

"I think we'll revisit this at a later date. You will have a lot of questions to answer, Miss Smith."

Christine Ryan cleared her throat. "Now, while this was happening, Mr. Kane was up country somewhere. Is that right?"

The Chinook touched down outside the French Peace-keeper camp and let me off. I walked down the ramp into the dust-riddled heat and headed toward the main gates. Inside was a hive of activity. A young officer walked over to me and asked, "Are you Kane?"

His accent was thick. "That's me."

"Follow me. I'll take you to the commandant."

As I followed him, I looked around. "What's the fuss about?"

"Some rebels have been seen in the area. We're preparing just in case they decide to attack us."

"Has it happened before?"

"Once."

The HQ was in a dugout lined with sandbags. "Commandant, this is Mr. Kane. Mr. Kane, Commandant Kilian Blanc."

I nodded. "Nice to meet you, sir."

"You too, Mr. Kane. Lieutenant, please fetch Captain Sarr."

"Yes, sir."

The lieutenant disappeared and Blanc said, "I am surprised, Mr. Kane, that you are here."

"Need to find out what is happening," I replied.

"I can tell you that. The rebels are everywhere. Their Russian advisers are no more advisers than I am an admiral, and we've been ordered out of the country."

I frowned. "First I've heard of it."

"It was announced by the new president. Anything remotely to do with the west has been ordered to leave."

"Sounds like a puppet to me."

"Indeed, it does."

There was movement behind me, and a woman wearing a uniform walked in. Blanc introduced her to me as Captain Ella Sarr.

We shook hands. "Nice to meet you."

"You, too."

"The captain will be your guide to where you're going. Take care of her, I'd hate to lose a good officer. You, on the other hand, I don't give a damn about."

"You have my word."

"Fine. I'll leave you in her capable hands."

We went back outside. In the sunlight, Sarr's blonde hair seemed to shine, and her skin darken. She put on sunglasses and said, "I'll just draw some things from the store."

"I'll need a weapon and some body armor," I said to her.

"Then follow me."

When we reached the stores, she grabbed me the body armor I requested and a Heckler and Koch USP handgun. She also drew me a HK 416, which matched her own weapon, along with extra ammunition. "Anything else?" she asked.

"Some frag grenades and NVGs?"

"I'll see what I can get."

Returning, she handed over the NVGs and grenades. "And?"

"Comms." I raised a hopeful eyebrow at her.

She sighed and went back. When she returned this time, she handed me my kit. "There."

"Thanks."

Sarr said, "Tell me, what are we doing?"

"There is a diamond mine I want to look at."

"The Kirefu Shimu?" she asked.

"I'm not sure of the name. No one has heard from the people up there."

"That will be the one. It is said to be under the control of the Russians."

"But what happened to the workers?"

"There was a mix of workers. Local and foreign. Like you said, no one knows anything."

"How do we get in?" I asked Sarr.

"I'll have a couple of my men take us so far, and the rest of the way will be on foot."

"Fine. Let's go."

"Before we do, I need to know what kind of man I'm working with. Have you had experience with this kind of thing?"

"On more than one occasion."

Her face turned grim. "I hope so, because there is a good chance we won't come back."

————

Knocker and Holly were in trouble. Gunfire was coming from their left and ahead of them from rebel soldiers and

Russian advisers. Knocker shot a Russian and pulled back behind some corrugated tin. "This is fucked."

Holly shot a careless rebel and took cover as well. A storm of bullets peppered their hide. Above the shanties of the slum, gunfire echoed for hundreds of meters. Knocker glanced from cover and saw two Russians moving right.

"Time to go. They're trying to flank us on the other side."

Holly reloaded. "I should never have got out of bed this morning."

Knocker turned away and said, "Moving."

Holly turned to join him. They started to navigate a narrow path lined with rusted dwellings. Each time they reached an intersection, Knocker would check it. Ahead of him were two men. "Move! Move!"

They took one look at him and pressed themselves against one of the walls. Gunfire erupted and forced Knocker to cower. One of the locals took rounds to his chest and legs before falling to the ground.

"Shit," Knocker growled. He leaned around the corner and fired. Holly was stopped behind him. "I'll cover you. You need to make the jump across there. Ready?"

"Ready."

Knocker stepped out into the open and fired his weapon. Behind him, Holly ran across the gap. Once she was across, he followed her. "Keep going, girl."

The slum was like a rabbit warren of paths, and an open area they reached at one point might have been a creek. Now it was a mess of black sludge full of rubbish and shit. But it was wide, and there was no way across.

"This way," Holly called out as she went left.

Knocker stuck close behind her.

"Try your cell again," Knocker said.

"It won't work, the networks are down."

"Why don't you have a sat phone?"

"I don't fucking know."

Up ahead was a bridge across the River Shit which they climbed up to and took it, continuing their hazardous trek. A few minutes later, Knocker realized that the sun was going down. "Hold up, I need a break."

"Too old?" Holly asked.

"Too many beers."

They found a vacant shanty and went inside. Holly looked at him and said, "How do we get out of this one, Raymond?"

Knocker grinned. "My dear old mum said to me once, Raymond, if you ever bite off more than you can chew, then chew like hell. That's exactly what I aim to do. Ammo check."

CHAPTER 6

SARR AND I REACHED THE LIMIT OF OUR RIDE NOT LONG before dark. When we climbed out of the transport, we started on foot. The going was hot even though the sun had gone down. We kept walking across the difficult terrain.

It was just after midnight when we reached the mine site. Even in the moonlight we could see the abhorrent scar it left on the landscape. Sarr said to me, "Most of the mine was dug by hand."

I was astounded that something so big could have been done so. Then she continued, "At the center is a deep pit with machinery in it."

"What is the ratio of locals to foreign workers?"

"From the reports I have read, mostly management positions are filled by foreign workers."

"Get some sleep. I'll take first watch. We'll have a look come daylight."

Sarr found a tree to lean against and was soon asleep. I liked that about her. No complaints, making the best of a situation. She took over from me three hours later, and when she woke me, the sun was rising above the horizon.

"Any dramas?" I asked.

"Quiet as a church."

After consuming some rations, we moved to where we could see the mine. The workers hurried over it like ants on a mound. Armed guards walked the perimeter and we saw no one else. I don't know if we expected to see any management or what. After an hour of watching, something happened that changed what we knew. A Russian guard called one of the workers over. They were soon joined by two more guards then things became animated. The guard shot the worker dead.

"What the fuck was that?" I said aloud.

As we watched, the guard bent down, looked over the dead man, took something from his body, and held it up to the sunlight before putting it into his own pocket.

"The worker was stealing," Sarr said.

"Pretty harsh punishment."

The other two guards carried the body away. I thought for a moment and then said, "Wait here. Keep your comms open. I'll be back."

"Where are you going, John?"

"I want to see where they bury him."

"Why?"

"I have a feeling the labor might not be the only ones in the ground."

Even though I left Sarr on her own, I had full confidence in her. I skirted the perimeter of the diamond mine until I found what I was looking for. The two guards were burying the worker among a number of graves.

Watching patiently, I waited for them to finish. The last thing I wanted was for them to know we were there. When they were finished, they went back to the mine.

The thick jungle provided good cover for me, and as I exited, I forced it aside. Approaching the graves, I counted numerous mounds, some freshly dug. Now, the trick was to find the right one.

The first was wrong. It was another native worker. However, the second grave produced fruit. As I scraped away the dirt, I saw what was once a white shirt. More removal and I found what I assumed was a mine manager. I took a photo and covered him back up.

"Sarr, can you hear me?"

"Loud and clear."

"I'm coming back to you," I informed her.

"Did you find something?"

"I did indeed."

I skirted the perimeter once more, heading in the opposite direction. Sarr was still in the same position. "You see much?"

She shook her head. "Not a great deal. Just working—"

She was interrupted by an inbound helicopter. We looked skyward and picked it up at a distance. It was an Mi-24. We watched it land, and as the rotors ran down, three people got out. Two were soldiers, one was a man in a suit. "That's interesting," Sarr said.

"It is if it's who I think it is," I replied.

For the next hour, the man in the suit was shown around the mine. I watched on intently as he'd stop, talk, then move on. Then, just before he left, a large box was loaded onto the helicopter. I said, "No prizes for guessing what was in that."

"You said you thought you knew who that was," Sarr said. "So, who is he?"

"I don't know."

She looked at me as though I was crazy, so I filled her in on what we knew.

"So, what are these so-called generals up to?"

"I don't know that either."

"Then, what now?" Sarr asked.

"I got a picture, so hopefully our people should be able to make something of it. Tell me about the aid convoy."

Sarr related the story to me and finished by saying, "It wasn't far from here."

"Close enough to have a look?"

"I guess so. No one has been that way since it happened. The convoys are forced to use an alternate route."

"Fine. Let's go."

———————

Meanwhile, Knocker and Holly had waited until dark the night before to keep moving. It was still fraught with danger because the searchers had brought in a helicopter with a spotlight.

They snaked their way between the shanties, trying not to draw attention to themselves. However, two armed personnel in a slum, running around at night, is bound to draw at least some attention.

"Hey," a voice said.

Knocker turned to see a man armed with a machete standing close. The dull light showed him to Knocker. The man was soon joined by three others, each of them was armed too. One with a machete and the other two with pieces of lumber wrapped in barbed wire which also had nails protruding from them.

"Not tonight, fellas," Knocker said. "I'm not in the mood."

"Then you will give us your weapons and we will let you go."

Knocker chuckled. "Mate, you and your friends go and find someone else to harass."

"The woman, she is nice, yes? You fuck her?"

Knocker remained silent.

The man said, "Yes, you fuck her. What is she like? Does she scream when you do it? Maybe I would like to make her scream."

"You're not very fucking smart, are you? You don't even have a gun."

"Maybe I don't need one."

There was something in his expression that triggered a warning. "Holly, behind us!"

It was the only place they could have been, and Knocker's warning was spot on. Holly brought up her 433 just as two men appeared with AK-47s.

"Contact rear," she called out and opened fire.

Knocker swung to meet the threat and took down the second would-be killer. The first was already down, thanks to Holly's quick reaction.

Knocker turned to face the other four men who were already closing in. If they'd had any sense, they would have run, but they didn't and paid the price.

The first guy with the machete wielded it as though it were an axe. Knocker used the 433 to block the blow and drew his Glock, pumping three shots into him. The man's spine arched under the impacts, and he staggered backward. The Glock came up higher and Knocker put one into the man's head.

The threats kept coming, and the Glock hammered once again. Two to the chest and the second threat was down. Holly took care of the next with a burst of fire from her weapon, and Knocker took care of the final would-be killer.

"That'll bring the shit down on us," he said. "Come on, let's get out of here."

Running through the narrow alleys, they eventually found their way back out. Knocker noticed a nearby vehicle on the side of the road. Running over to it he opened the door, noticing a key in the ignition. "Come on. We've got a ride."

He turned around to see if Holly was coming, but she wasn't there. "Holly?"

When there was no response, he hurried back across the

street and found the 433 lying on the shoulder. Knocker looked around and called out again. "Holly?"

But there was still nothing. "Damn it."

Running back across the road to the vehicle, Knocker climbed in. Then he drove back to the safehouse.

"You abandoned her just like that?" Holland asked with a tone.

"There was nothing I could do except go back to the safehouse and get help."

"But they could have raped her, killed her even."

"They didn't."

"Tell us what happened."

The first thing Holly knew about her kidnapping was the hand closing over her mouth. She tried to scream, but the grip that held her was unbreakable. She was dragged back into the darkness. The last thing she saw was Knocker looking in the vehicle across the street.

One of her captors took her weapon and left it on the shoulder. Her handgun was confiscated by another of her kidnappers.

Shortly after that, Holly was put into the back of a van and driven to a large rundown compound on the outskirts of Kinshasa. A hood had been placed over her head, but Holly had the sense to remain calm. She would need all her strength to get through this, and a beating from her captors would only drain that strength away.

When the vehicle stopped, Holly was dragged from the van and taken inside the compound. Forced onto a chair, her hood was removed. She took in the dimly lit room and then looked at the man seated on a larger chair facing her. He stared with penetrating eyes.

Holly summed him up in one sweep. Forties, egotistical, dangerous. He said, "Who are you?"

"Holly Smith."

The man chuckled. "I am Smith too. Victor Smith. Welcome to my home."

"Why have you done this to me?" Holly asked.

"Because I can and because maybe your country will pay money for you."

"This is a kidnap for ransom?"

"Something like that," Victor replied with a flick of his wrist.

"What if they don't?"

"They will, or you will die." The reply was succinct.

"Who is Victor Smith?" German asked. "The report gives his name but not who he is."

Holly replied, "A local mobster who ran a lot of illegal trade in Kinshasa."

"Violent and sadistic prick," Knocker said. "Liked to cut pieces off people to get his point across. One time, he killed a rival's son. Cut him up in little pieces and spread him over the rival's lawn."

"Charming," said Christine Ryan.

"Psycho."

Holly waited to see what he would do next. When he remained silent, she said, "How will you know where to send the ransom demand? It won't be the embassy because it is shut down."

"You will tell me."

There was a struggle at the door and a man was brought in between two armed guards. He was forced to his knees in front of Victor. The mobster said, "Holly, this is Damien. He is an American aid worker from Idaho. We asked Damien's family—nicely of course—for five million dollars for his safe return. They haven't paid, so alas, he must."

Victor's right hand was empty, then it wasn't. In it was a small pair of pruners. One of Victor's guards grabbed Damien's hand, holding it out while the other held him steady. Victor walked over to him and said, "I am truly sorry, my friend. However, this will hurt you more than me."

The howl of pain was blood-curdling as it echoed

throughout the room. Holly closed her eyes, not wanting to see. After he was done Victor stood up and said, "There, all done. I will see you tomorrow."

Damien was dragged away a whimpering mess. Holly looked at Victor and said, "You are a fucking animal."

He shrugged. "I am a businessman. But now you see what will happen if no one pays."

She glared angrily as he gave her a cold, mirthless smile. Victor continued. "My men will return shortly and show you to your accommodation. I trust you will be comfortable with your stay."

The fucker was psycho. He drew pleasure from what he was doing. Holly had no doubt that neither Damien nor herself would ever see freedom again. Unless Knocker could do something about it.

———

"Hey, Ray, join us for a beer," Lincoln said as Knocker walked through the hotel foyer around midnight.

"Fuck off," he growled and kept walking.

"Whoa, someone needs to go to bed."

Knocker found Foster and said, "We have a problem."

"What?" he asked, half asleep.

Knocker told him, and the man came fully awake. "Christ. Sounds like she's been kidnapped."

"Not the Russians?"

The MI6 man shook his head. "No, if it had been them, they would have shot you too. This will be Victor."

"Who the fuck is Victor?"

"Come in, I'll get the others."

Five minutes later, the rest of the MI6 team was gathered. Knocker went back to his question. "Who is Victor?"

Foster said, "Victor Smith. Thinks he's a big-time mobster. All he amounts to is a murderous thug. Kidnaps foreigners off the street and ransoms them, most of the time —shit, all of the time—he kills them anyway. His favorite pastime is dismemberment."

"Will he rape her?" Knocker asked.

"Not until the end. I figure we have twenty-four hours before things start to happen."

"What do you mean?"

"Well, he's going to reach out to her family. She doesn't have any, so that will kill the money issue. And she won't compromise her MI6 cover, so that puts us on the clock."

"Shit," Knocker growled.

"Don't worry. We'll find her, you just have to get her out."

"Piece of piss."

———

Holly was fetched from her basement cell just after dawn. She'd spent the rest of the night trying to sleep, but the various moaning and sobbing noises emanating from Damien's cell had made it difficult.

They returned her to the room where Victor was waiting for her. "I hope you slept well," he said.

"Like a log."

He stared at her, a half-smile on his face. "I like you. Now, down to business. I need contact details for your family."

"I don't have any," Holly replied.

He frowned. "No details?"

"No family."

"Then what are you doing in Kinshasa?"

"On holiday."

Victor's voice grew harsh. "This is how it works. I ask the questions and you answer truthfully. Understand?"

Holly nodded. "I am here working with BritAid."

"Now, that is better. I will contact them and organize for your release."

"They won't pay you. They don't have that much money."

"I'm sure they will be able to find it."

"I'm not," Holly replied. She figured it would take BritAid time to figure out if she was even an employee, which was in her favor.

"For your sake, I hope so. As for poor Damien, his family cannot pay. They offered me one hundred thousand dollars for him. Can you believe it? An insult. Not to me but for Damien. Obviously they do not think his life is worth much."

"Just let him go," Holly suggested.

Victor shook his head solemnly. "Alas, I cannot do that. Insults like that must have a price."

As had happened the night before, Damien was brought in between two guards. This time, there was no fight left in him. He just stood with a hangdog expression, a guard on either side of him, waiting for Victor to talk.

Victor said, "I am sorry, my friend. It would seem that your family does not think enough of you. It was an insult. And insults like that must be paid for."

He nodded to a third man who was standing in the room. For the first time, Holly noticed that this man was wearing a leather apron. He walked toward Damien holding something in his hand.

Holly stared at it for a moment, thinking that she was seeing things. Then she realized she wasn't. The man was holding an electric circular wood-cutting saw.

"What are you doing?" she stammered.

"I am sending his family a message," Victor said.

"You can't do this."

"I can do anything I want." He didn't look at her when he replied.

Holly looked horrified. "This is inhumane. You are crazy."

Victor stared at her for a moment. "Then maybe this will give you something to think about. Because if I don't get money for you, this is what is in your future."

He nodded to his man. The guard on either side held out the arms of their prisoner. Holly closed her eyes. The circular saw screamed to life. The guard holding it stepped forward and started on Damien.

Holly fainted.

When she eventually came to, Damien was dead. His body parts had been taken away. All that was left on the cold, hard floor was a pool of cherry-red blood. Holly leaned over and vomited. After she'd emptied the contents of her stomach on the floor, she sat up and wiped her mouth.

"Do you feel better now?" asked Victor.

"You—you're a fucking animal."

"You can go back to your cell now. I'm still waiting to hear from the aid agency. I shall have you brought before me once I know more."

CHAPTER 7

THE DAY WAS ALREADY STEAMY AND GETTING WORSE BY THE time we reached where the convoy had been ambushed. There was nothing left to see except a few spent cartridges lying on the ground. In our travels, we'd come past a water hole and seen a variety of animals, including an Okapi, a pride of lions lazing about, and even a leopard in a tree eating its fresh kill.

"What happened to them all?" I asked Sarr.

"We assume they were killed."

"If they were they would be buried around here somewhere. Let's have a quick look."

We scouted around in a broad circle for thirty minutes before Sarr found something. She called me over, and when I got there, I saw what she'd found. The mounds were unmistakable.

"They buried them," she said.

"Yeah."

We stood in silence for a while, the only sounds were those of the jungle.

At least at first.

"Do you hear it?" Sarr asked.

I nodded. There was gunfire in the distance. "It can't be too far. Let's take a look."

We made our way through the brush toward the popping sound. We must have walked a mile before we came upon it. It was a rebel camp. Not just any rebel camp. It was huge. As we lay there on the hill overlooking it, I said to Sarr, "There has to be at least two thousand rebels down there."

"At least," she agreed.

Then I pointed something else out. "Do you see the trucks?"

Sarr nodded. "They're going somewhere."

"Do you think they would attack your FOB?"

She shook her head. "I don't know, but if they do, there's more than enough of them to overwhelm it."

I took a photo. "I agree. We need to get back to talk to your commanding officer."

"Will still have to walk a fair distance before we can get transport out," Sarr said.

"Let's hope nothing happens before then," I replied. "Come on, let's get out of here."

———

We walked for the best part of the day before we came across the train tracks. "What are these?"

"They are for one of the mines. If we follow them, we can make the small station further on and be picked up from there."

"Well, follow the yellow brick road."

We traversed the rail line until dark, crossing a river on a high trestle bridge. After two more kilometers, we came across the outstation. From what I could gather, it was just a stop along the line where supplies could be loaded and unloaded from outlying farms. On a short siding there was a steam train with four boxcars and a flatbed. We went inside the station but found no one there.

Sarr said, "It looks like it's been abandoned."

"See if you can get us that ride."

I looked around but found nothing. By the time I came back, Sarr had already organized for someone to come and pick us up. "We've got three hours."

I nodded. "Get some sleep. I'll take first watch."

She found a corner to huddle into. Closed her eyes and I could hear her breathing even out after only a couple of minutes. This woman was good.

––––––––

It wasn't till just after dark that the MI6 people found out where Holly was. Foster called Knocker into his room and said, "We think we've located her. There is a compound just outside the city. We're reasonably certain that Victor and his people are there."

"Do we have photos or anything like that?" Knocker asked.

"We're working on it. But if she is there and we want to get her out, we need to go tonight. Which will mean possibly going in blind."

"Just point me in the right direction, chief, and turn me loose."

"Give me an hour to try to sort things out," Foster said. "Just be ready to go."

So for the next thirty minutes, the MI6 people pored through documents and photos, trying to get the lay of the land. Once they were done, Foster came back to Knocker.

"This is what we have," he said, showing him a satellite photo. "We've marked the guards, but we've no idea how many on the inside. I'll drive you, and then it's up to you to get her out. I'll wait outside the perimeter for you."

"Just get me there," Knocker told him. "I'll make sure this fucker never sees the light of day again."

"We leave just as soon as you are ready."

So, Knocker prepared himself, ammo'd up, full kit, NVGs included, and went and did what he does best. Kill bad guys.

———

They stopped outside the compound on the eastern side. Foster had an MP5 fully loaded and ready to use just in case he needed it. There were fires still burning in the city from small pockets of resistance. There was an orange glow in the sky to the west. Foster said, "Are you good to go?"

"Just try to be here when I get back. And keep the comms channel open," Knocker said as he pulled the mask down.

"I'll be here, Jensen. Count on it."

Knocker cut his way through the fence and waited in the shadows for the first guard. The man appeared a minute or so after Knocker breached. Two bullets and the first man was down and out of the fight. Then Knocker really went to work.

The second guard was standing beside a brick wall. By the time he died, his brains were on it. The third was near an empty pool with three big cracks in it. He was dead in the bottom, three bullets in his chest and another in his head.

The fourth guard died when Knocker cut his throat. He'd hidden in some bushes until the guard went past, then opened his throat with his knife.

Number five was shot like the others. Having a cigarette beside an overgrown pergola, the man died with a well-placed bullet to the back of his head. Six was on the roof of the building, prowling like a cat looking for a target.

Knocker killed him with one accurate shot. The man hadn't even made a sound. Seven and eight were chatting near the vehicles the goons had used. Knocker used his knife on the first man. Came up behind him, clamped his hand over his mouth and stabbed him several times in the chest before opening his throat. The other guard was killed with Knocker's suppressed Glock.

That left one more, a guard at the back of the house. Knocker crept around there and found him smoking as he sat on a lawn chair. The guy deserved to get what was coming to him. But instead, Knocker came up behind him, clamped a hand over his mouth, and pressed the suppressor against the back of his head.

"Do you understand English?"

"Hmph."

"Just nod, motherfucker, or shake your head. Try anything else and I'll paint the grass with your brains."

He nodded.

"Where is the English woman?"

Knocker loosened his grip. "Basement," came the muffled reply.

"How many inside?"

"Five."

"Where is Victor?"

"Bedroom."

"Where?"

"Back of the house."

"Thanks," Knocker said and then shot him. "Foster, I'm going inside."

"Good luck," Foster replied.

"Yeah, they'll need it."

Knocker chose the easiest route into the house. Through the front door. Before entering, he reloaded the Glock and put a round up the spout. Opening the door slowly, he eased inside. For a guy who was supposedly rolling in money, the man's house was shit.

There were two ways he could play this, Knocker figured. He could go straight to the basement and get Holly out, or he could clean house first. He chose the latter.

First room on the right. WHAP! WHAP! The suppressed Glock did its work. Second room on the left. Another bad guy sent to meet the devil.

Knocker moved fluidly like an avenging angel floating above the floorboards. According to the guard, there should be three more. He could hear voices in the living room. Two men were watching the television.

The first one he shot in the back of the head. Brains and blood blew over the television screen and seemed to slide down like a macabre curtain. The second guy yelped but died almost instantly after as he tried to get to his feet.

"One asshole left," Knocker muttered.

Locating the room he needed, Knocker placed his ear against the door. There were sounds emanating from the other side, but Knocker was unsure about what he was hearing. Then he realized. He swung the door open and saw the man hanging from the ceiling while the naked woman whipped him. Knocker could see the blood streaks among the scars on his back. "Well, fuck me."

The woman let out a yelp and turned to see the intruder. She dropped the whip and backed away from Victor. The mobster couldn't move. Knocker looked at the woman and said, "Get out."

She left the room in a rush just as naked as the day she was born. "What is going on?" Victor demanded.

Knocker walked around him and stared into his face. "Hello, Victor."

"Who are you? Let me down."

"No. As for who I am, you can call me…" He thought for a moment. "You can call me the Vindicator."

"What?"

"Don't like it? Oh well. I'm here to get a friend of mine. Holly Smith."

"She is in the basement. Let me down."

"No."

Victor started shouting for his men.

Deciding to have some fun, Knocker shot him in the leg. The killer howled in pain. Knocker said, "Don't worry about your men. They're all dead. Put down like the fucking animals they are."

"You cannot do this," Victor hissed.

"Before we finish, tell me about the whipping. You like that? Does it make your cock hard?"

Victor snorted and snarled, foam starting to form at the corners of his mouth. Knocker continued his torment. "What happens then? Do you get all worked up and prematurely ejaculate before you can get it in? Mate, you are really fucked up."

Victor heaved at his restraints, trying to break free. "I will kill you, white man. I will cut bits off you and leave them for your family to find. Just Like I did—"

WHAP!

Knocker shot him and it was done.

He looked around to make sure there were no further threats, he then went down to the basement. "Holly?"

Silence.

"Holly?"

"Raymond?"

"Yeah."

"Over here."

Crossing the room to the far corner, he found her in the shadows, crouching down to remove her bonds. She fell into his arms, relieved her predicament was over. "I am glad you are here. We'd best leave before someone comes."

"No one is coming," he told her. "They're all dead."

"All of them?"

"Yeah."

"Oh, okay."

"Foster, we're coming out."

When they reached the SUV five minutes later, Foster was relieved to see them. He said, "Something is wrong."

"What do you mean?"

"I can't raise anyone from the hotel."

"Then let's go find out what's wrong."

"Did you have any idea about what happened?" Christine Ryan asked.

"No, ma'am," Knocker replied. "No one could have predicted what we found."

"Do you believe it was your fault?"

"How could it be our fault?" I asked.

"I wasn't asking you, Mr. Kane."

"I gave you an answer."

When Knocker and the others arrived back at the hotel, it was like a bloodbath. Bodies were strewn everywhere. Reporters, staff, and the MI6 team. All had been shot dead, some even hacked up with machetes.

"Who did this?" Holly gasped.

"Rebels," Foster answered.

"But why?"

Knocker looked around at some of the corpses. "There's more to this."

"What do you mean?" Foster asked, the shock of what he was seeing starting to set in.

"I've seen rebel carnage in African countries, and this doesn't feel right. I need to see security footage."

"You are kidding, right?" Foster demanded.

"No. Do you have it in your suite?"

"Of course."

When they arrived at the suite, they found it in a state of devastation. Every piece of equipment that had previously been hidden there was wrecked or gone. Knocker looked around. "Rebels don't go after equipment like this."

"The security footage we had set up is gone," Foster said.

"Then we try the hotel's," Knocker said, heading for the door.

It took a few minutes to reach the back of house office, which served as the security hub of the hotel, and they found the system there in the same state as the one in the suite. They found the manager of the hotel dead behind his desk.

"This is just crazy," Holly said. "Why kill all these people?"

Knocker looked at the equipment a little closer. "Hello," he said.

"What?"

He held up an SD card. "When you smash things, you need to make sure you do a decent job of it. They smashed up the hard drive on the recording system but forgot about the backup. I just hope it has something on it."

"All we need is something to play it on," Foster said.

"Why aren't there any police here?" Holly asked.

"There are no police, no civilians on the street, nothing."

They went out to where all the journalists had been killed. Knocker sifted through the wreckage and found a laptop in a case. "Let's try this."

Opening it, he was relieved to see it spring to life. However, there was one snag. It was password protected and they couldn't get access. Looking at Holly, he asked, "Can you?"

She took it and stared at the screen. Then she worked her magic by hitting a sequence of keys which unlocked it straight away. "I'm impressed," Knocker said.

"Don't be. After 9/11, the intelligence world got together, and that code was one of the things they came up with. They had a hacker placed at Microsoft and he managed to put a backdoor into every computer system they manufactured. What you think is secure, is, but only to those who don't know the code."

"Big Brother's dollars hard at work."

"It has saved a lot of countries against terror attacks and allowed us to make the world a safer place."

While she spoke, she danced her fingers over the keys. Then the files appeared, and she started them playing. The first was earlier in the day. The third was the one they were looking for. The first sign of trouble was a porter running through the main doors, a scared expression on his face. He hadn't made it far before falling forward as though pushed by an invisible hand.

Moments later, the cause of the porter's fall walked through the door. An armed man wearing a hood. He was followed by others. Chaos ensued.

Foster said, "They look like terrorists."

As the feed flicked through different camera feeds, Knocker said, "Freeze there."

It stopped on one of the shooters.

"Since when do terrorists use Russian SR-3s?"

"You're right. They were Russian," Foster said. "But Russian what? And what were they doing?"

Knocker looked at Holly. "Looking for us."

She nodded. "They had to be. It's all about the camera."

"Why, what did you do?" Foster asked.

"We took a picture of a guy at the press conference that Elia held. Someone saw us and they wanted it. That was how we ended up in the predicament we were in."

"But who is he?" Foster wanted to know.

Knocker nodded at the screen. "Him."

"Who is he?"

"No idea."

"Then we need to find out."

"I'm guessing he's dead," Knocker said.

Foster frowned. "What do you mean?"

"Not literally," Holly clarified. She gave him a quick rundown before saying, "We need another place to stay and wait for John."

Foster countered with, "No, we get out. I can get us on a ship and out of the country in under twenty-four hours."

"I'm not leaving Reaper," Knocker said.

"I'll get word to him, but in the meantime, we go. These people didn't find you, that means they won't stop."

Holly touched Knocker on the arm. "He's right."

Knocker grunted. "Fine."

"I think we'll have a break about now," Holland said.

I nodded and stood up from the table. I stretched out the kinks and said, "Give us twenty minutes or so. We'll head to the canteen and get something to eat."

"Very well."

Knocker, Holly, and I headed toward the cafeteria, selecting food and a drink from the fridge before sitting at a table. Knocker looked at me and said, "This bites, just like yesterday."

I nodded. "Holly, what were you asked about yesterday?"

"I was questioned about my decisions and decision-making. I'm thinking that once this inquiry is over, I'm going to be out of a job."

Knocker gave her one of his broad smiles. "It's not that bad. Ask us, we're already out of a job."

I shook my head and gave her a wry grin. "You're alive, take it as a win."

Ten minutes later, we were back in the room with our interrogators. "Okay, before we get back to the ship incident, let's go to what happened to Mr. Kane," German said. "I'm not condoning what you did, but this was like something out of a movie."

———

We were picked up after the three hours and taken back to the French FOB, greeted by Commandant Blanc, who was still organizing his troops in preparation for the withdrawal. When we broke the news to him, he told us we were wrong.

"Why would they attack us?"

"Why would they murder the foreigners at the mine? Why would they ambush the convoy and kill them all?"

"You said you have pictures?"

"Yes." I showed him the photos I had.

He nodded. "So, there are rebels in a training camp."

"There are around two thousand of them, Commandant. How many do you have?" I knew he had under a hundred men and women. "You need to get you people together and get out of here now?"

"And go where?"

"Do you have a map?"

He walked to the wall shelf and collected a roll, unfurling it onto his desk. I leaned over and looked, stabbing my finger at the map. "Angola."

"That is two thousand kilometers away. How do you expect us to get there?"

"By train."

"You're out of your mind. Where could we possibly get a train from?"

"Where we were picked up."

"John, you don't even know if it works," Sarr pointed out.

"You have mechanics, don't you?" I asked.

"Yes, but—"

"If we stay here, we die. I mean—"

"Sir," a young soldier burst in.

"What is it?" Blanc demanded. "I'm busy."

"Sir, Captain Sarr had us monitor an area northwest of here for activity."

Blanc glared at Sarr. "Did she?"

"Yes, sir."

"And?"

"We've picked up a force of—well, I'm not sure who they are—but they're moving."

"In which direction?"

"This way, sir."

"Very well. I want all of the officers here as soon as possible and the troops mustered on the parade ground at dawn."

"Yes, sir."

Blanc looked at me and Sarr. "It would seem that you were right, and I was wrong. However, getting back to your train would seem to be on a collision course with the rebels coming to us."

He was right, but I wasn't beat just yet. "Sir, if you let me take Captain Sarr, a couple of your mechanics, and ten of your soldiers, we could head back, try to get the train moving, and meet you…there. Just this side of that river."

"If I agree to that, Mr. Kane, you would have maybe two hours before the rebels reached the out station."

"Yes, sir, it would be tight. But that's if they go that way." Once more, I touched the map. "There are two routes that they could take. The one where we'll be or this one here."

"That's a big gamble."

"Yes, sir, but with a little luck, we'll be gone before they get there anyway."

"All right. Is there anything else you will need?"

"Just a couple of things."

CHAPTER 8

WE HEADED BACK TO THE STATION WITH THE ITEMS WE thought we might require. Luckily, one of the mechanics, Remy, was a train fanatic, and although he'd never operated one before, he had a thing for engines.

While another couple of men worked on the train, I sent out a two-man patrol and we gathered wood for the boiler of the locomotive. Old sleepers were dry and would burn perfectly.

There was also water in the large water tank to fill the train, but first, it had to be going. That meant building up steam and even getting some water into it before we could top it off.

I designated others to load some sandbags onto the flatcar behind which we placed two mortars and a light machine gun. I figured that once we got rolling, two soldiers in the driver's compartment would be enough for security.

Sarr found me when I was helping load the railway sleepers. "We're making fine progress."

I looked at the smoke coming from the train stack. "Were they able to get some water into the boiler?"

She nodded. "Remy is about to try to move it to the water tower."

The train started to chuff, and I glanced toward it. Dark smoke billowed from the stack and into the air. At first there was nothing, and then it slowly crept forward. I smiled, any movement was something. Sarr rested a hand on my shoulder. "Was there ever a doubt?"

Voices became raised as Remy barked orders at those with him. The locomotive moved forward until it cleared the points and then backed up under the water tower. The boiler was filled, and then the loco was moved back into position to be attached to the boxcars and flatbed.

I looked at my watch. The preparations had been fruitful but had still taken too long. And as if to confirm it, the two men who were sent out of forward patrol came running back. "Rebels. Coming this way."

"How many?"

"Maybe a hundred."

"How far, man?"

"They will be here in five minutes."

"Okay." I turned and called to Remy, "How long, Remy?"

"Ten minutes."

"You don't have that long."

"Yes, sir."

I thought for a moment. The rebels would have to cross a reasonable patch of open ground to get to us. We had two LMGs. One was on the flatbed, the other was—

"Sarr, get that other LMG setup over near the station. Put another man with him. They are to stay out of sight until I give the word. Just like the others. I'll be on the flatbed."

"We can't defeat that many, John."

"I don't want to. We just need to make them hesitate for a bit."

We hurriedly organized to receive the incoming rebels.

Remy and the other mechanic prepared the train for departure. I was on the flatbed, crouched behind the sandbags. Both the two-man mortar crews were doing the same.

It was almost five minutes later when the first rebels appeared along the narrow road, all on foot. But they weren't alone. The group was accompanied by a couple of Russian advisers. My guess was that they had been ordered to look over the out station.

They came in slowly, cautiously. I mean, what would be more suspicious. A train billowing smoke and a flatbed with sandbag fortifications. But I had a plan for that. I looked at the man beside me and nodded.

With a yelp, he jumped up, leaped down from the flatbed, and ran across the open ground toward the station house.

There were shouts from some of the rebels and they surged forward at the thought of the blood sport they were about to be involved in. Behind them, their Russian advisers called for them to halt, but they kept running.

I looked at the mortar crews. "Do it."

They leaped up and dropped their first rounds. Soon, both were arcing forward to land within the oncoming rebel column. My job was operating the LMG. I opened fire just as the first rounds from the mortars hit.

Rebels scattered left and right. Some were cut down in the twin blasts. As the mortar team continued a steady rhythm, I continued to work the LMG.

Rebels dropped out in the open. Some were dead, others were trying to use the ground as cover and started to return fire.

The other French soldiers worked their own weapons with precision practice, and the surprise ambush had the desired effect, for as more mortar rounds rained down, the rebels leaped to their feet and headed into the bush.

I saw Sarr run over to the locomotive where Remy was

working. Then she ran along the train to where I was. She climbed onto the flatbed and crouched beside me. "Remy is ready."

"Good, get everyone aboard."

Sarr disappeared, and soon, the scattered few of the French soldiers were running across the open ground toward the boxcars. It was at that time that the rebels chose to attack again.

They came out of the bush howling like wild beasts, firing as they came. I opened up with the LMG again, aiming low for the kick-up as the weapon fired. More mortar rounds cut holes in their advance but still they came.

"Sir, we're running out of mortar bombs," one of the loaders called.

"Just keep going," I called over.

A few moments later I heard both crews call, rounds complete. They were out of ammunition, and still, the rebels came on.

The second LMG was operated by a big man named Bear. His real name was Bevis. Seeing the plight of having no more mortar ammunition, the big man broke cover and used his LMG like it was a garden hose, scything left and right as bullets cracked all around him. His selfless act provided cover for the others to reach the train. However, with a lot of selfless acts, especially one like Bear was performing, they have consequences. Sometimes dire ones. It proved that when two rounds brought the big man to his knees.

"Shit." I jumped down from the boxcar and ran across to where Bear was on his knees. "Come on, big man, you can't stop here."

Sarr joined us. Between the three of us, we made a nice fat target. Bear was weakening fast, and instead of trying to get up, he lay down.

He looked up at Sarr and said, "I am sorry, Captain, I cannot do it."

I grabbed the LMG. "We need to go now. He's done."

"We cannot leave him."

"He's done, Sarr, now get your ass on the fucking train."

She emitted a low, frustrated growl before running for the train. I took one last look at Bear and said, "Sorry, pal."

Blood was coming from the corner of his mouth now and he nodded understanding and closed his eyes. Then I followed Sarr to the train.

I tossed the LMG to a young soldier in a boxcar door and ran toward the flatbed. The train was already starting to move torturously forward. I climbed up onto the flatcar and jumped behind the sandbags.

The mortar crews were now firing their personal assault weapons. One had grabbed the LMG. They were pouring a steady rate of fire into the oncoming rebels, their path marked by the bodies behind the leaders.

The train jerked again, and it began to pick up speed until, eventually, the distance was growing as we pulled away and started toward the rendezvous.

Remy had the train moving well. It would take an hour to get to the rendezvous where the rest of the French force was waiting. I climbed from the flatbed up onto the roof of a boxcar. I made my way along to the next one before climbing down the rungs near the main door that was open. One of the French soldiers helped me in, and I looked around for Sarr. She was standing off to one side on her own.

"It was the only thing we could do," I told her.

"He was still alive. God knows what they will do to him."

"No, he died just before I left," I lied. It was the right thing to do because I needed her focused. "Was Bear the only one?"

"Yes."

"Then we were lucky. When we reach the rendezvous, the mortars will need more ammo, so too the LMGs."

"We should put snipers on top of each boxcar," Sarr said to me.

"I agree. But at the moment, two might do."

She went over to her men, tapped two on the shoulder, and said, "You two, up on top. Keep your eyes open."

She came back over to me. "I hope the commandant is ready when we get there."

The tracks wound around hills and across creeks and a river before we reached the rendezvous. As hoped, Blanc had all his men and women there. He looked pleased to see the train but had bad news anyway. "We will have no help. Headquarters have said there will be no air cover, so we are on our own. All the rest are being pulled out."

We told him of the brief battle and the loss of Bear. He nodded and said, "He was a good sergeant. And a good man. We can grieve him later. Let's get the train ready."

The train was loaded with all the spare ammo, water, and food. We were looking at maybe two days to get there traveling the back rails and trying to stay away from major centers. Providing the tracks were usable.

There were two fifty caliber Browning Machineguns brought along as well. One replaced the LMG on the flatcar, and the second was fixed to the roof of the second boxcar. Meanwhile there was movement at one of the trucks. Then I saw what they were doing. Two FGM-148 Javelins were loaded onto the flatbed.

"I thought you guys were peacekeepers," I said to Sarr.

"We were until things hotted up. We managed to acquire some other weapons. They wouldn't let us have helicopter gunships."

Blanc found us a few minutes later. "We are ready to go."

"Then let's go."

"Did any information come to light why the rebels chose to attack that company of peacekeepers?" Jack Holland asked.

"They were directed to by Elia under the orders of Noskov. I can only assume that I was the target. Somehow, they knew I was there. Judging by how complex their intelligence system was, it wasn't surprising. The same with Knocker and Holly. We found out they hit Victor's place not long after Knocker rescued Holly. Assumedly to get her.

"Once more, we were getting too close to what they were doing. We'd discovered their oil secret but didn't stop it. Now we were onto their diamond scheme and had laid eyes on another of their group. We knew Shatov and what he looked like. Just not where he was located. We knew of the one we called The Russian but didn't have a name for him. Then there was the third one in the DRC. We'd come up against dangerous organizations before in our work, but these people were something else. Their intelligence gathering was exceptional."

"Okay, carry on."

We continued south along the rails for another twenty kilometers before reaching the first junction. The train stopped, and I went forward with Blanc and Sarr.

"Which way?" Remy asked.

"Take the left," I said.

Remy looked at the line and then at Blanc. "Sir?"

The line was overgrown and hadn't been used for years. There was no telling what kind of disrepair it had fallen into, but the other way was out. Blanc looked at me and said, "Are you sure that is wise?"

I shrugged my heavy shoulders. "It doesn't matter if it is or not. If we go the other way, we are sure to head through one of the bigger towns, and now they know we're on the train, they'll be looking for us there. Traveling these old lines is the only way."

"Sir?" asked Remy again.

Blanc eyed him and said, "Get us on the other line. But keep our speed down, just in case."

The next six hours were spent traveling slowly, stopping constantly, checking rails and bridges. About two hours before dark, things came to a grinding halt when we reached a trestle bridge.

The train stopped, and I, along with Blanc, Sarr, Remy, and a strong-jawed sergeant major named Bartholmieu Roy, climbed down and started out on foot. It was halfway across the structure that we started to find broken timbers beneath the rails.

Remy shook his head. "That will not hold the weight of the train."

"Then we have to make it so it can," Blanc said.

Remy thought for a moment. "Maybe we could brace it somehow. It might hold then."

"Do what you have to do, Remy."

"Yes, sir."

"Sergeant Major Roy, set up an OP on the far side of the bridge. Send out a small patrol to look around. Order them to go no more than a mile."

"Yes, sir."

"Captain Sarr, we'll set up another OP three hundred meters back along the track. They will be replaced every two hours."

"Yes, sir."

"How far do you figure we have come, Mr. Kane?"

"Three hundred kilometers, maybe."

"It's going to take us forever to get out of here," Blanc said.

"Have you got a map?"

Blanc nodded and found his map, spreading it out so we could look it over. He was right. At this pace, we were screwed. My eyes ran over the names and places, and I found what I was looking for. "Here. See this village?"

"Yes, what about it?"

"When I was operating here as a Recon Marine there was an airfield there. It is big enough to put a C-130 down. If you can talk to someone in your head shed and get them to send a bird, then we can forget Angola."

"They said they won't enter the airspace."

"Not with air support. This is an extraction," I pointed out.

"How far is it?"

"Another two hundred kilometers by rail and then maybe a day on foot."

"It looks like we'll be traversing some savanna. Could be a problem out in the open."

"Then we do it at night."

He nodded stiffly. "You get us there, Mr. Kane. I will get us a flight out."

———

An hour before dark, two things happened that almost brought everything crashing down. The first was the helicopter. Audible before we could see it, the WHOP-WHOP-WHOP of the rotor blades echoed along the valley as it grew closer.

Blanc ran over to me. "It's coming this way."

"Yeah, tell Remy to get the train moving across the bridge. The trees on the other side should be enough cover."

Blanc started barking orders at his men. "Sarr, order the OP to take cover. Everyone across the bridge now. Remy, get this thing moving."

"We don't know if it will hold, Commandant."

"You're about to find out." He climbed up. "If the bridge collapses, we go together."

"That instills me with a lot of faith, Commandant."

Blanc slapped him on the back. "We'll talk about it later."

I jogged ahead of the train with Sarr. The helicopter could still be heard as it flew closer. It wouldn't be long before it was on top of us and it would radio back our position. Then, without doubt, it would attack.

The hard part about running across a trestle bridge is the fact that, in some places, there is nothing beneath you.

Behind us, the train started moving. It crept forward, but at the pace it was going, the helicopter would have been and gone before they got halfway. Besides, the slower the pace, the more time the weight of the train spent on the weak part of the bridge. Blanc must have realized this and ordered Remy to go faster.

By the time we reached the other side of the trestle bridge, the train had gathered speed. I heard the creaking and cracking as it crossed the damaged section, but it held. They had done their work well. Then it was across and pulling under the thick tree canopy which would hide it. Except for the smoke. We could only hope that they thought it was from a fire.

The helicopter appeared low overhead as it streaked toward the north. I waited, listening to see if it was going to come back. It didn't.

"Captain Sarr, get everyone loaded up. We move now."

"Commandant, a word," I said.

He looked at me and nodded. We moved out of earshot. "What is it, Mr. Kane?"

"What is it you propose to do when dark comes?"

He sighed. "We'll have to stop. If we come across another bridge like this one, we won't know anything is wrong with it until we're plunging to our deaths."

I nodded in agreement. "Then continue in the morning."

"It's the only way."

"If you need me to do anything, Commandant, I'm here."

"Mr. Kane, if anything happens to me, I would like you to take command."

"No, I couldn't do that to Sarr. I will try to guide her though, if she needs it."

He nodded. "Thank you."

CHAPTER 9

KNOCKER AND HOLLY ARRIVED AT THE PORT OF BOMA, climbing from the SUV with Foster under the cover of darkness. On the dock, they met with the captain just before the ship was due to sail. He was an Englishman, a former navy man with twenty years' experience in the Royal Navy before transferring over to drive *box lorries*, as he called them.

"You just made it," Les Ingram said. "We were just about to throw lines and head out."

"Thanks, Les. I owe you big on this one."

"Anything I can help with?"

"Not at the moment. Do you still carry an anti-pirate team aboard?"

"Wouldn't set sail without one," he replied. "Am I going to need them?"

"I hope not. Who is your team leader? Anyone I know?"

"Former SAS man. Pete Jones."

"I know him," Knocker said. "Good man. Came across him in the Regiment. Do you mind if I talk to him?"

"Not a bit. You'll find him in the mess. Anyway, we should all board. We'll be out at sea by dawn."

Once aboard, Knocker worked his way to the mess, where he found five men seated around a table, playing cards. Knocker looked at the table next to them, where their weapons leaned, ready to go at a moment's notice.

A tall man with a beard looked up and grinned. "Of all the pricks you least expect to see on a ship, you'd be the last one I'd expect."

"Yeah, well, we can't all be unlucky," Knocker replied.

"What are you doing here anyway?"

"Mate, we're up to our armpits in the shite. If I were you lads, I'd be ready for anything."

Jones's face grew stern. "That bad, huh?"

"These people don't fuck around."

"Then if they poke their heads up, we'll show them we don't either. You want a coffee?"

"Sure, why not?"

Jones got Knocker a coffee and introduced his people. Apart from Jones, there was Stevens, Lewis, Young, and Carter. All had served. SBS, SAS, and Commandos. Jones sat down across from Knocker. "I hear you've been busy these past years."

Knocker shrugged. "You know how it is."

They talked for a while before Knocker excused himself and went to find Holly. She had been put in an isolated cabin with its own facilities for her comfort. When he knocked and called her name, she opened the door and let him in. He sat down in a chair. "How are you doing?" he asked.

"I'm...okay," she replied hesitantly. "What about you?"

"Me? I'm good. This shit happens to me all the time. Well, me and Reaper."

"You know he'll be all right."

"Yeah, just makes me wonder where he is and what he's up to."

Holly nodded. "I can't say I'll be happy until we're out in the Atlantic."

"Yeah, me too."

While the train had stopped for the night, the ship continued along the Congo toward the Atlantic, vibrations humming through the ship's hull. Knocker was on deck in the darkness, watching the outline of the tree-lined bank slide past. It would be daylight in a couple of hours, and he would be forced below deck.

He glanced at the illuminated face of his watch. There would still be seven more hours traversing the Congo before slipping out into the Atlantic. "Couldn't sleep?" Holly asked as she came up behind him.

"Nope. Too much going on in my head," Knocker replied.

"Me too," Holly said. "I think it's the vibrations."

"Yeah, they take a bit of getting used to."

"I've been trying to work out our next step when we get out of here," Holly said.

"Try to figure out who our friend was?"

"Yes. That would be a start. But this is such a mess."

"You're preaching to the choir, lass."

"Why are they so invested in the DRC?" Holly asked.

"I was thinking about that myself. Although we won't know anything until Reaper returns, I think the outstanding word you used is invested."

"Money?"

"Diamonds. But yes, ultimately money."

"What's your point?"

"Let's think about it for a moment. Their collective name. The Gods of War. What does that say?"

"We know they are generals, or former generals," Holly said.

"Yes."

"Right, now does the UK have anything like them? A secret group that if you had to say they were Gods of War, who would it be?"

"Some kind of think tank scenario runners."

"Exactly."

Holly paused. "I think I'm with you, Raymond, but lead me to the next step so I can confirm it."

"What are some of the big things you need to start a war?"

"Weapons, oil…and money. Shite, are you saying that they're planning for war?"

"Did you tell anyone about this theory?" German asked, inter-rupting.

Knocker shook his head. "No. It was just a theory. What kind of pillock would I have looked going off crying wolf without anything to back it up?"

Knocker shrugged. "I don't know what I'm saying. However, these bastards have just come into a lot of oil. Now they're acquiring the wealth they'll need. I mean, let's face it, as far as riches go, Russia is pretty fucked at the moment. And to cap it off, they've just put a hardliner into power at the Kremlin. They're trying awful hard to stop us from finding out something."

"But NATO wouldn't stand for their aggression if they attacked another country," Holly pointed out.

"Like I said, I don't know what I'm saying. But they're up to something."

Holly was about to speak when Knocker's hand on her arm stopped her. She looked at him, the concern on his face evident in the mix of moonlight and ship lights. "What is it?"

"Wait."

At first there was nothing. Then something became audible. Knocker turned to Holly. "Helicopters. Warn the captain. He should have a safe room for himself and the crew. Go."

"What about you?"

"I'm going to find Jones. Get in the safe room with the others. Tell the captain no alarms."

Knocker went to the mess first but found nothing. Then he remembered that they had their own quarters, so he headed there instead.

Holly found Ingram on the bridge. Foster was with him as the two talked about how the world used to be. Foster saw her and said, "It looks like I wasn't the only one who couldn't sleep."

"Jensen sent me up here. There are helicopters inbound and he said we should all get into the safe room." She looked at Ingram. "Do you have a safe room?"

He nodded. "Yes. I'll sound the alarm."

"No, don't. He said not to."

"Fine. I'll do it another way."

Ingram made a call through the ship's internal communications system. When he was done, he turned to the bridge crew and said, "Set all failsafes and let's go."

"Wait, who's going to drive this thing?"

"The satellite."

"Shit."

Then as Holly looked out through the window toward the bow of the ship, she saw the helicopter hovering as its passengers started to rappel to the deck. "They're here."

———

Knocker found Jones and his men and they were now gearing up, ready to meet the threat. Jones had a spare kit and gave Knocker some body armor, an M6A2, and extra ammunition. To Knocker's disappointment, they had no frag grenades. But they did have flashbangs.

Jones asked, "Are these the people who are after you?"

"Most likely. Remember, they're good."

"So are we."

They headed up to the deck and arrived just as both helicopters peeled away. The second had unloaded its passengers at the stern. They would be going for the bridge.

Knocker tapped Jones on the shoulder. "Your call."

"Bow first, then the bridge."

The team pressed forward, Knocker bringing up the rear. The point man made contact with the first enemy shooter as he came around a deck-stored container. Suppressed rounds smashed into the steel sides of the box and screamed off into the darkness. Jones's man took a ricochet to the throat and fell to the deck as his life pumped out of him.

"Fuck, Lewis," Jones snarled and opened fire at the shooter. The rounds hammered into the shooter and the intruder fell dead to the deck.

Jones's team split in two. Knocker tacked on with Jones and Young. They worked their way between a couple of container stacks and then, at the end, they paused. Jones looked around the end and pulled back. He held up two fingers. Young nodded and they both broke cover, weapons up, and ready to fire.

THWAP-THWAP!

THWAP-THWAP!

Both intruders fell. Jones and Young dragged their lifeless bodies into the shadows. Jones turned to Knocker. "You going to do anything?"

"Sod off. You guys have it all under control."

Bullets cracked around them soon after the words escaped his lips. They dropped to knees, and all three opened fire at the man cutting loose from atop a blue container with a large Maersk sign stenciled onto it. He disappeared backward from the container, bullets in his head and throat, and crashed to the deck.

Knocker heard Carter say over the comms, "Skipper, two down, port side. The rest of the bow this side is clear."

"Roger that. Clear the bridge."

So, they all headed back along the deck toward the bridge structure.

Gunfire erupted from the superstructure. But it wasn't Knocker and those with him taking fire. It was the other team. For a moment the comms was silent, then a pained voice said, "Skipper, Carter is down. I'm wounded and pinned down this side."

"Shit," Jones growled.

Knocker said, "Go. I'll retake the bridge."

"Not on your own, mate."

"Leave it with me. It's what I do."

"Shit, Knocker, watch your ass."

Knocker hurried aft toward the bridge structure. When he reached the first ladder up, there was a sentry posted at the bottom. The M6 in Knocker's hands came up and he shot the man twice. The sentry staggered and Knocker closed the distance between them.

He took out his handgun and shot him in the head. The man flopped to the deck, lifeless at the bottom of the stairs.

Knocker started up, his weapon aimed at the landing on the first level. As soon as his boot touched the landing, gunfire rattled out and bullets ricocheted around him. He threw himself to the deck and felt a bullet glance off his body armor. He rolled and came up shooting. The would-be killer staggered back and slammed against the rail before tipping backward over it and disappearing to the deck below.

Knocker began climbing the second flight of stairs. He moved slowly, not wanting to hurry headlong into a storm of bullets with his name on them. Reaching the landing, he was relieved that no one had tried to kill him. Knocker then hurried to the base of the third flight, which would take him to the bridge.

"Knocker, you there?"

"Roger that," Knocker replied as his boot touched the first step.

"I'm coming to you. Give me a location."

"Approaching the bridge, port side."

"Roger."

Knocker kept low when he reached the landing at the bridge. He pressed his back to the cold steel of the exterior just below one of the windows. Knocker rose cautiously and peered inside. The bridge was empty. "Where are you assholes?" he muttered.

He crawled over to the rail and looked out across the deck below. He could see no one which meant they were inside somewhere, searching for their targets.

"Jones, the bridge is clear. If there is anyone left, they're below deck looking for targets."

"Knocker, I checked out one of the dead guys. They're definitely Russian. Another thing, he had charges on him."

Knocker thought for a moment and then said, "The safe room. They know about it."

"Meet me on the deck."

Knocker hurried down the stairs and found Jones waiting for him. "Follow me, Knocker."

He let Jones lead the way, and minutes later, they were moving through a warren of passageways below deck. Then they heard the voices. Jones peered around the corner and saw four men placing breaching charges on the safe room door. He drew back and said, "Four of them placing charges."

Knocker swapped positions with Jones and took a look for himself. He saw what they were doing, and being experienced in breaching from his time with the SAS, he knew they were using too much explosive.

He pulled back, took out the partially used magazine, and replaced it with a fresh one. Jones asked, "What are you doing?"

In the dim light, Jones saw Knocker wink at him. He shook his head. "Jesus Christ."

Knocker stepped out into the hallway and started shooting.

Two rounds for each target.

Eight rounds altogether.

Four dead men.

Moments later, the saferoom opened and Holly appeared. "They were the last four, Raymond. We were tracking things from inside."

Ingram appeared. "Well done, Mr. Jones."

"Yes, sir. I need to see to my men."

"Casualties?"

"Two dead, one wounded."

"I'm sorry."

"They knew the risks, sir."

Ingram nodded. "Quite. Have our doctor take a look at your wounded. Let's get out of here."

———

We were now on foot. The company was strung out, walking through the savanna bush toward the airfield. Our path was illuminated by moonlight. The night was cool. Much cooler than the day had been. I heard a lion roar to the south of us. Every now and then there were other animal sounds, but nothing close enough for concern.

We humped in relative silence. It would be dawn soon and we would need a place to hole up. I was on point with Sarr. She walked behind me without a word. I waited a few steps until she fell in beside me. I said, "We'll need a place to lay up."

"There is a water hole ahead of us. What about there?"

"No. Animals will be around it. Somewhere away from them. I think I can see a large stand of trees ahead of us. We'll stop there."

"I'll let the commandant know."

The thicket when we reached it was perfect. I lay on the ground near a tall tree with a thick trunk and broad canopy. Minutes later, with my weapon lying beside me, I was asleep.

Not long after sunup, however, I was awake again. I had been in a deep sleep when things kept hitting my face. At first, I thought it was flies. I swatted at my face and brushed them away. But they kept coming. Once more, I swatted them away from my face and grunted my disapproval as I opened my eyes. Then, in the tree above me, I saw the problem. Not everyone can say they went to sleep and woke up with a leopard staring down at them.

I froze, not knowing what to do. It was then I realized that Sarr was asleep beside me. "Sarr?"

She kept sleeping.

"Sarr?"

"Mmm?"

"I think we need to move."

"Why?" she asked as she rolled over to look at me.

"Because there is a leopard in the tree above us."

"Uh-huh."

The leopard must have sensed something for it came down out of the tree like forked lightning. I grabbed at my sidearm, but the big cat was on the ground and gone before I could do anything. It was a good thing he wasn't after one of us.

"You weren't being funny, were you?" Sarr said, rolling

over to see where the creature had gone, not sure that anyone would believe her if she told the story.

"Not hardly."

We were about to lie back down when the small spotter plane appeared. It came in low over the landscape, sounding like an angry bee. Men scattered everywhere and I cursed at what had just happened. There was no way known that they could have missed us.

I ran to where Blanc stood. "That's torn it."

He nodded. "There is only one thing for it. We have to keep moving."

The company formed up and we started toward the airstrip. The sun was hot and the flies were thick. Blown was the option of resting through the day. Gone to the northeast with the spotter plane.

An hour after we'd left the thicket, Blanc came to me. "I am thinking of sending a small force out front to go ahead and secure the airstrip. I would like you to lead it."

I nodded. "Do you have any objections to me taking Sarr with me?"

"No. Have her pick the ten volunteers to go with you."

It was a good thing to do...pick volunteers. "We'll head out in five minutes."

Sarr selected the ten men to go with us. One was a sergeant named Levett. He was an experienced soldier, having been in for ten years. The younger men looked up to him and they looked to him for guidance. He was the right fit for the patrol.

We pushed hard toward the airfield through the heat and the humidity. Everyone kept up a good pace, some of them stretching even me. We took a short break every hour before pushing hard again.

Approaching the airstrip using the cover of a dry creek bed, we saw it opened out onto the plain short of the airstrip itself. Leaving the soldiers in the bottom of the creek bed, Sarr and I eased up to the edge and took in all before us.

"How many you think?" Sarr asked.

It was hard to tell. I tried to do a rough calculation but couldn't come up with a definitive number. "Maybe thirty," I said.

"It looks as though they dropped some men in as a welcoming committee," Sarr said. "They look to be Russian."

"Waiting for us. I bet there is a big force coming up behind Blanc to drive him onto this spike."

"What do you want to do?"

"Kill them all."

CHAPTER 10

My knife slid between the Russian's ribs, and he died silently with my hand fixed securely over his mouth. I put him out of sight under the truck near the old hangar. Somewhere nearby, Levett was doing the same. We'd circled the airstrip and came up behind it through the bush. Sarr was holding the rest of the group back, ready to sweep in and take out the Russians.

But first, Levett and I would clear a path. There was another guard on the roof of the hangar. I moved quickly to the ladder and started to climb, hoping that it wouldn't rattle or squeak and give my presence away.

As I neared the top, I slowed my momentum and peered over the edge through the rungs of the ladder. The Russian was looking out across the airstrip instead of in the direction he should have been.

The distance I had to cover was great enough to be troubling but close enough to be a possibility of getting it done. I took the shot and climbed onto the rooftop. My HK416 was up and centered on my target. If he turned now, I would have to shoot him. But he never did.

As I approached, cat-footed across the structure, he

seemed to be in a trance, staring across the strip. I lowered the 416, letting it hang by the strap before taking my knife once more and ending the man's life.

Lowering him to the rooftop, I hurried back to the other side, signaling to Sarr to bring the rest of the group forward. Surprise mattered. Without it, there was a good chance the plan would fail.

Levett climbed the ladder. We would act as snipers while the others began the attempt to overwhelm the Russian force. Once in position, we started the ball rolling and opened fire.

My first target was a man in a makeshift machine-gun-pit. My bullet punched into his skull, and I saw the red stain appear on the sandbags behind him. Beside me, Levett took his target.

Then Sarr attacked with her force and battle was joined.

As targets appeared, I picked them off, having taken down two more Russians before I saw one of the French soldiers go down wounded in the leg. A Russian raced toward him, intent on a kill, but a 5.56 round from the 416 I held dropped him at the Frenchman's feet.

The soldier looked in my direction before dragging himself back behind a truck and taking cover. I could see Sarr. She had her weapon up and firing. For a moment she barked an order, and the soldier on her right moved away from her toward a small shed.

The French were good, well-trained, and at the top of their game. The Russians, on the other hand, were lazy, and the surprise attack gave us the upper hand. Gunshots rattled out, lifting in intensity as we pressed home our attack.

One by one, the Russians fell under withering fire. But we didn't have it all our own way. Apart from the soldier I'd seen wounded, we'd had another two wounded and one killed.

Then the gunfire stopped. Most of the Russians were

down. A couple had surrendered. Many had died, but there were wounded. I climbed down and said to Sarr, "Reach out to Blanc. Tell him what has happened and that we need the extract sooner if possible."

"What are you going to do?"

"Talk to the prisoners."

There were two of them. The only ones who weren't wounded. I took pictures of them with my cell and asked, "Who are you?"

The biggest of the two said, "Fred and Barney."

"I see you like cartoons," I replied. "I'll ask again. Who are you?"

"Rocky and Bullwinkle, motherfucker."

So, I hit him. Reversed the 416 and hit him with the butt between the eyes. He staggered and went down on one knee. I looked at his friend, and without even asking him, he said, "Andrey. I am Andrey and he is Ilya."

His friend hissed at him.

I stared at them for a moment. "Are you dead?"

He knew what I meant but feigned ignorance. "No, I'm alive."

"You know what I mean. Are you dead?"

"Do I look dead?"

"Okay. How about this. Do you work for them?"

"Who?"

"The generals?" I replied.

"I am a soldier. Of course, I work for generals."

"The Gods of War?"

His eyes flared and then went back to normal. "I don't know what you're talking about."

"You're lying to me."

"If you say so."

Short of torturing what I wanted out of him, I was going to get nothing. Sarr came back and said, "Blanc is twenty minutes out. He's got company following."

"What about the plane?"

"Thirty minutes. It's going to be cutting it fine."

"I need Levett."

"Sure, what are you going to do?"

I said, "I'd like to organize a little reception."

"Take him. Just be careful."

I found Levett near the hangar. I said to him, "Want to give me a hand?"

"What are we doing?"

"Make some bombs. Ever heard of a man named MacGyver?"

Levett shook his head.

I grinned. "Come on, you'll love this. Grab a couple of your guys and follow me."

We worked solidly for the next fifteen minutes, grabbing some old drainpipe we could use and gas out of the trucks. We rigged them on the approaches and then set up trip-wires for those we missed.

Blanc appeared and I sent Levett to guide them around the killing zone we'd set up. When he reached me, he said, "You've been busy."

"Almost done. Can I borrow your mortars and the LMGs?"

"Take what you need."

"Thanks. Have your people set up in a line across this side of the runway. There is a ditch there which will afford you some cover."

"Let's hope your plan, whatever it is, works."

"How many?" I asked.

"Two hundred, maybe more."

"They should have brought more."

Blanc moved his soldiers into position with a couple of snipers on top of the hangar. The radio lit up with the incoming C-130, but the pilot's voice sounded urgent. As he'd been approaching, he'd seen the incoming force of rebels. Blanc told him to hold his position until he ordered him in.

A few minutes later, the rebels appeared. As I watched them, they weren't going where I needed them to be. They were too far right. They would need some guidance. I ran across to the hastily prepared mortar pit. The man in charge was a young corporal. I said, "When I tell you to, I want you to drop three rounds to the right of the rebels. I don't want them scattered. I want them moving in. Don't put any rounds among them. Not yet. Understand?"

"Yes, sir."

We waited. Everyone was under orders to hold their fire until ordered to do so. The rebels came cautiously forward, and moments later, I said, "Now, three rounds."

Within a few heartbeats, there were two rounds in the air and one sliding down the tube. As requested, the rounds landed exactly where I wanted them. At first nothing happened. The rebels sped up, coming straight ahead. "Give them two more rounds."

An additional two left the tube. This time, the effect was instant. They pushed across toward the kill zone. My face was grim. "One more."

The soldier fired, and the round nudged the rebels across. I slapped the corporal on the shoulder.

"When the signal goes up, burn through what you have. Right on top of them."

"What is the signal?"

"Don't worry, there will be no mistaking it. You can't miss it."

I ran forward into the ditch, landing beside Levett. "Okay, let's light them up."

The line on either side of me in the ditch opened fire. But not everyone. We needed to have the rebels think that the center of the line was it, making them attack through the kill zone.

When the firing started, they paused, going to the ground. Then, with the minimal staccato sound coming from the center, one of them became braver. He was followed by a second, then a third, and before long, they were all coming straight at us.

It had been a long shot, but it worked. I turned to Levett. With a nod I said, "Do it."

Moments later, the gas-filled pipes exploded with a roar, engulfing the rebels. Human candles staggered around as they burned. It was an awful way to die, but in times like this, as they say, better them than you.

The explosions were the signal for the rest of the line to open fire. Both rifle and LMG fire ripped across the open ground toward the surviving rebels. The mortars joined in along with the snipers on the hangar, and soon, rebels were dropping like tenpins at a bowling alley.

Some tried to escape the killing zone and ran into the tripwires rigged by Levett and myself. More fell as chaos and panic reigned. It was like sharks amid a killing frenzy with blood in the water. We were outnumbered and outgunned, but that didn't last long.

The remaining rebels turned and ran. Among them, I saw two Russian advisers trying to hold them together. But it was no use. The tide had turned and there was no stopping the rebels as they ran.

Firing ceased a few moments later. It dwindled then died away completely. I turned to Levett. "Tell your commandant to get his plane in here now, before anything else happens."

Sarr came over to me. Her eyes were wide, and she was pumped up on adrenaline. "That was crazy."

"Better them than us," I replied. "Just remember, if they get hold of you, especially you, they would have raped you and then killed you. Maybe cut your breasts off just for the fun of it."

"It doesn't mean I have to like it."

I nodded. "No, it doesn't."

Minutes later, the C-130 was on the ground, its loading ramp lowering as it taxied. Five minutes after that, everyone was aboard. The casualty count from the airfield battle was one scraped knee where a soldier had tripped on a rock. We were lucky. Now we were getting out.

But some of us would be going back.

"If you ask me, you were more than lucky," German said. "You and Mr. Jensen seem to have the lives of a cat or the luck of the Irish. I'm not sure which."

"I suppose you could look at it that way."

"Why would you want to go back?" Christine Ryan asked. "Your mission was a bust, and all you could look forward to was a firing squad."

"We weren't done," Knocker replied for me. "We were asked to go back in, and we said yes. Besides, at that time, Lazar Noskov was still in the country, and he was a target of interest."

I said, "If we could get him, it would go a long way to putting some pieces of the puzzle together. If not the whole damn thing."

"So, facing death, you went back anyway," Christine Ryan said, raising an eyebrow.

"A little dramatic, but yes."

"You're brave men, I'll give that to you. Brave or crazy."

Knocker grinned. "You don't have to be crazy, ma'am. But it sure as shit helps."

"Quite, Mr. Jensen."

Cape Town was where we regrouped for a week before Holly came to us with a plan. Well not quite a plan, more like a request. Over the week we'd been in the city the DRC had started to settle. Peacekeeping forces had been pulled out of the country, and more Russian advisers had moved in. Intel sources had the mining sector of the DRC taken over by Russian companies for a percentage of the profits. Except for the diamond mines.

That was a different scenario altogether, as we were about to find out. Holly came to the room we were using for briefings and had a folder tucked under her arm. "Is that the naughty book?" Knocker asked with a grin.

"By the time I'm done, you'll wish it was," she said to us. Placing it on the table, she opened it. "Okay, first things first. Lazar Noskov. Former commander of the Russian 35th Army. Dropped off the face of the earth in 1995 after a supposed plane crash in Siberia. Last seen in the DRC."

Knocker said, "These assholes look pretty good for dead people. We now know two of them. Two of, according to your friend Georgy, five generals."

"Yes. Are you feeling up to another mission?"

"Sure," I replied.

"Okay. The British government wants to get Arthur Kayembe out of where he's being held. They came to us to do it."

"You mean some prick volunteered us to do it," Knocker said. "Was it that prick Short?"

"You don't have to go," Holly said.

"You know we'll go," I replied. "Unfinished business."

"Maybe so, but Kayembe is the prime target."

"Why do they want him out?"

"To save face," Holly replied.

"Is Noskov still in the DRC?"

"Like I said, that was the last place he was seen."

"You do know, if he pops his head up, I'm going to chop it off, right?" I said.

"I understand."

"Fine. When do we go back to the DRC?"

"Once we have the support elements in place. You'll insert by parachute drop. Extract will be by helicopter flown into Kinshasa from across the river in the Republic. Whatever happens in the interim is up to you."

I reached out and took the folder. The second picture looked to be an old police station in the outer parts of Kinshasa. "What's this?"

"This is where he's being held. It is what it looks like. An old police station surrounded by chain wire fence with barbed wire on top. It has been taken over by the Russians. The mission is time-sensitive because we believe that they intend to transport him to Russia."

"Why would they do that?" I asked.

"Because while he's in the country, there is a chance his supporters will rally, and things will get out of hand again."

"So, we get him out before they transport him."

"Yes. There are two days to prepare. You will be transferred to the Republic on the third day and go the next night."

"How many Russians on-site?" I asked.

"Intel has maybe fifteen or twenty X-Rays within the perimeter."

"That's a lot for two men to handle," I pointed out.

"I didn't say it was going to be easy."

I grunted. "It never is."

Holly left Knocker and me to go over the intel. We looked at aerial photos and decided the best way in was from the back of the compound. Cut the fence and gain access through the hole. The key was stealth. Sure, we would have to take down the guards, but anything else would have to be avoided if possible. The main point of worry was the closest area a helicopter could put down was one kilometer east of where we were. It looked like a football pitch. Knocker shook his head. "If we get Kayembe out in one piece, we have to get him to the extract. If he's in poor condition, we might as well shoot him and ourselves inside the fucking police station."

"Yeah, it is a bastard of a hump. There is a creek in between with only one bridge. We could risk the creek, but who knows if there would be crocs in there from the river."

"We have to be spot on with our jump," Knocker pointed out.

"Uh-huh. Not to mention our timing. If we're late, we'll have Russians breathing down our necks. If they're late, we're screwed."

"You really have to love some of the shit we volunteer to do," Knocker said. "One day, we'll bite off more than we can chew and break our teeth on it."

Slapping him on the shoulder, I said, "Get masticating."

Knocker looked aghast at me and said, "Keep your personal problems to yourself."

I laughed and said, "Masticating is another word for chewing."

"I knew that, but I wish you would use normal words."

————

I found Holly later that evening. She was drinking beer in the hotel bar. Knocker, for some strange reason, chose to forgo beer for a book he was reading. I checked to see if he was all right, and he said he was but that he was slowing down in his later years.

"How did you go with the intel?" Holly asked.

"There are a few things that need ironing out, but—beer, please, pal," I said to the barman. "But we should be able to get it done. Say, did you want another beer?"

She smiled at me. "No, I'm fine for the moment."

"How are you doing after your Kinshasa experience?" I asked her.

Holly gave an indifferent shrug. "I won't lie, I was scared. But Raymond saved the day."

"He has a habit of doing that. He's a good man to have beside you when your back is against the wall."

"How long have you known him?"

"A while. We've fought some together."

"Global, right?"

"Even before that. We've lost some good friends over the intervening years."

"Why haven't you got out?" Holly asked.

I took a sip of my beer. "I keep trying but something always seems to reel me back in. I think I'm starting to become resigned to the fact that one day I'll pick up a mission and I won't come back."

"That's a bleak way of looking at it."

"It's a bleak profession," I replied.

She stared at me before finishing her beer and placing the glass on the bar. Holly held out her hand and said, "Come on, walk me back to my room."

I stared at her curiously for a moment before she pulled me to my feet. I winced, and she said, "Few kinks?"

"Yeah, something like that."

"Maybe I can fix them for you too."

Holly sat on my buttocks as she used her palms and knuckles to work out the knots in my muscles. She'd taken some oil out of the cupboard in her bathroom and poured it on my back. I was stripped down to my underwear, and so was she. It was a royal blue. Nothing fancy, just practical. "Where did you get the Reaper tattoo, John?"

"Got it when I was in the Marines."

"Did you get the bullet holes there too?"

She got another knot, and a groan escaped my lips. "No, they're from all over."

"Uh, huh. Roll over."

I did as I was ordered. Who wouldn't? From there, things kind of popped up.

Once we were done, we lay there staring at the ceiling, the fan whirling above us like an inverted helicopter.

"What is the next step?" I asked.

"You mean after we get Kayembe out?"

"Yes."

"I'm not sure? I know you want to go after Noskov, but to do that, we need to draw him out."

I thought for a moment. "Can you track the diamonds?"

"We can try," Holly said. "Why?"

"I'll let you know. There might be a way we can draw Noskov out."

"Out of the DRC?"

"Yes."

"I hope so. If we could roll him up, it would be a great catch."

"Yes, now, I have to go."

Holly placed a hand on my chest. "Not yet, I still have a few more kinks to iron out."

CHAPTER 11

We had to drop on the football pitch. We were armed with suppressed M6A2s and Glock handguns. Knocker and I both carried fragmentation grenades as well as flashbangs. The plan, however, was still stealth.

"Now I know how the boys at Arnhem felt," Knocker said to me.

Arnhem was an airborne raid performed by the US 82nd and 101st Airborne Division and the British 1st Airborne Division reinforced by a Polish Brigade in World War Two, 1944. The Brits had been forced to drop on an LZ a good distance from the bridge they were meant to capture. What followed was disaster.

"Let's hope we have more luck than them," I said quietly. Although, things were off to a good start because there was no one around. Admittedly, it was two in the morning. But dropping in an urban zone was sketchy at best. "You ready?"

"Yeah."

"Home Base, Ghosts One and Two are down. Proceeding to target."

"Roger, Ghost One. Good hunting. Out."

I took point. Our first target was the bridge. To get

across the creek, we had to cross the bridge, and if there was anyone there, it would throw a wrench in the works. Our boots crunched on grit as we moved, and it sounded loud in the night air.

Reaching an intersection lit by orange streetlamps, I paused, knowing that we had to pass beneath them to keep going.

"What is it, Reaper?" Knocker asked.

"The lights."

"Lit up like London's East End."

"Yeah. What do you think?"

Knocker raised his weapon and swept left to right. "Can't see anything."

I raised my weapon and fired. The streetlamp shattered with a pop and the light went out. "Let's go."

We hurried through the intersection and along the gravel backstreet toward the bridge that crossed the creek. Suddenly headlights appeared, and we deviated from the side of the street to a dark alley near us. We crouched down until the vehicle roared past, not slowing at all. We came erect and pressed on. I noticed I was starting to sweat due to the high humidity that assaulted us even though it was dark.

Ahead of us now was the bridge. We were coming up on it fast, and it appeared to be clear.

But it wasn't.

There were two armed men, both pacing back and forth. We had to make another decision. Risk the creek and possible crocodiles or take the two men on the bridge.

Knocker said, "I'd rather take a bullet than become croc food."

"Me, too."

Moving forward stealthily until we were in a better position, we brought our weapons up and sighted on the two armed men. "Now."

WHAP!

WHAP!

Both dropped like stones into a heap in the center of the bridge. We ran forward, dragged them to the side, and heaved them over into the water below. Maybe they'd become crocodile food, maybe not.

On the other side of the bridge, we broke to our right so we could approach the police station from the rear. A dirt road ran along the back fence. The area was dark, a lack of streetlighting in the area to illuminate it. We dropped our NVGs down and turned the laser sights on for our M6s.

The road was uneven and potholed. In the darkness it would have been possible for either one of us to easily roll an ankle, but the night vision gave us the edge, including the sentry walking the back fence.

We waited for him to disappear, and Knocker hurried to the chain-link fence and started to cut it open. He'd only just begun when the sentry reappeared. "Knocker, hold, danger close," I warned him through our comms.

He dropped to the ground and remained still. Meanwhile, I had my M6 up and was tracking the sentry as he walked along the fence line. If he saw Knocker, there was going to be a problem. I would have to shoot him, but to do that, the round would have to pass through the fence. And the gaps weren't that big. The bullet only had to clip one strand of heavy gauge wire and the round would be deflected.

The sentry walked on.

He came abreast of Knocker's position and kept walking. A long breath slowly released from my lungs, and I realized that I'd been holding it in. Once the sentry was gone, I said, "Knocker, clear."

He finished what he was doing and slipped inside the compound. However, instead of waiting for me, he swiftly moved to the shadows of the building. I, on the other hand, waited.

The sentry reappeared and started his journey back along the fence. Then something struck me. I said hurriedly, "Knocker, stand down."

The armed man walked past the position where Knocker hid in the darkness and kept going. Once he had his back to me, I crouched low and started toward the hole in the fence. He disappeared around the corner, and I squeezed through the hole in the chain link.

From there, I ran across the open area and into the shadows.

"What the fuck, Reaper?" Knocker whispered.

"He's not walking all the way around. Which means he's meeting someone on the other side." I needed to say no more as he put it together. If he didn't meet up with the second sentry, the one on the other side would get suspicious. Then he would come looking, find his friend gone, and raise the alarm.

We approached the side door and tried it. It clicked open and we went inside. Both of us had drawn our suppressed Glocks and were ready to do whatever it took to accomplish our mission.

I hadn't gone far before I was forced to shoot my first Russian soldier. Then, no sooner had he found the floor when another appeared, and I shot him in the head too.

Knocker and I cleared the inside of the station room by room. By the time we were finished, we'd killed four more men. That meant we'd accounted for six inside. That was a lot less than the projected fifteen or twenty. The pleasing part, if there can be one about killing your fellow man, was that we hadn't triggered any alarms.

"Let's find him and get out," I whispered to Knocker.

We searched the cells but found them empty. "Shit. Home Base, this is Ghost One."

"Go ahead, Ghost One."

"Base, there is no bird in the nest. Repeat, no bird in the nest. It's a dry hole, over."

"He should be there, One," Holly replied. "All the intel says he's there."

"Well, he's fucking not," I hissed.

"Shit. Get out now. The helicopter will be there to pick you up soon."

"Roger that."

We exited the same way we'd come in. Once more, the sentry was walking past. Knocker touched my arm and slipped out behind the sentry. Moments later, the man was unconscious after a savage blow from the Brit's Glock.

"What are you doing?" I hissed at him.

"I didn't come all this way to go home with fuck all, Reaper. Maybe he knows where Kayembe is."

"We don't have time for this," I pointed out.

"Just help me get him out of here."

I muttered a curse and grabbed hold of the unconscious man. We managed to get him outside the perimeter and into the darkness, away from the police station. We lay him down and pinned him so when he woke up, he couldn't move. Knocker poured water over the guard's face and the Russian came awake. He struggled to get up.

"Alright, cock, just listen. You try anything, I'll kill you. Understand?"

The Russian stopped moving.

"I'll take that as a yes. Now, where is Kayembe?"

The man lay there, breathing heavy, the air sounding like snorts as it was drawn in and out of his nose.

"I'll ask once more. Where is Kayembe?"

Still nothing.

Knocker clamped a hand over the man's mouth and shot him in the leg. The Russian bucked and strained, his scream muffled by the palm clamped over his face.

"Once more you have tortured a man—"

Knocker stared hard at Jack Holland. *"I'd call it forceful inter-rogation. We needed information in a hurry."*

"Call it what you want. The shoe still fits."

"Grow up, Jack," Christine Ryan snapped. *"You know some-times the lines are blurred. You are no angel. Besides, we're not here for that. This is about the big picture. If we need to pass anything on to the proper department after that then we will."*

Holland glared at her.

"Continue, Mr. Kane," Christine Ryan said. *"I'm interested in what happened next."*

Knocker released his hand and said, "Now, where is Kayembe?"

"S-Sudan."

"Where?"

"Khartoum."

"Where in Khartoum?" Knocker whispered harshly.

"Pogibel."

"Be fucked," I whispered. "Ask him again. Make sure."

Knocker asked again, and the answer was the same.

"Pogibel."

"What is Pogibel?" German asked.

I opened my mouth to speak when Christine Ryan said, *"Perdition."*

"Yes, ma'am, that's right."

"I thought they were just rumors," she said softly.

"No, ma'am."

"What are you talking about?" German asked.

"When I was working at MI6 there were all kinds of rumors circulating about secret Russian prisons across the globe. Mostly in countries they had a lot of influence over. When I heard about purgatory, I thought nothing of it. Now there is Perdition."

"You can add Gehenna to that list and Hades," Knocker said. "But there are more."

"Unbelievable," the shocked woman replied. "And all these are run by the Russian system?"

"No, ma'am," I replied. "We believe they were all run by the generals themselves. Or under their influence anyway."

"Unbelievable. What happened next?"

I stared at the others on the panel then my gaze went back to Christine Ryan. "You won't like it."

"Tell me."

I shot the Russian in the head. We couldn't leave him alive because he would tell them what we were doing. With that done, I looked at Knocker and said, "Move your fucking ass."

We ran from where we were to the bridge over the creek. In the background, a siren started to wail. I guess they had found the dead inside the station. The bridge was still clear, so we ran across it and started along the street. "Home Base, from Ghost One."

"Go ahead, Ghost One."

"That helicopter better be on time because things are getting noisy on the ground."

"The bird will be there, One."

We kept running, our tortured lungs threatening to burst. As we got closer to the pitch, we could hear the helicopter. I looked up and saw the light in the dark sky. We'd been lucky so far and all we could hope for was that our luck would hold.

As we ran onto the pitch, the helicopter, a Chinook, touched down, its ramp already lowering. We jumped up onto it and jogged inside. The loadmaster looked around and said to me, "Where is the other one? We were told three."

"Not there. Only two of us."

The loadmaster said something into his boom mic, and almost instantly, the Chinook lifted into the air. Knocker and I sat down and strapped ourselves in, cursing that another mission was a bust.

———

"Are you sure he is in Sudan?" Holly asked me.

"Yes, Khartoum. That's what the Russian told us."

"Damn it. Where?"

"He said Perdition."

I waited.

Nothing happened.

Holly stared at me and said, "Is that supposed to mean something to me?"

"You've never heard the rumor?" I asked.

"What rumor?"

Knocker said, "Over the years, there have been rumors that the Russians had hell-hole prisons across the globe where they hid certain prisoners. When I was in purgatory, I never thought much of it."

"Neither did I," I said.

Knocker continued. "But this one is called Perdition, and it's starting to look like the rumors were true."

"Two prisons don't make a conspiracy," Holly pointed out.

"I think in this case it does."

"I'll look into it."

"Yes, ma'am."

"Meanwhile we have to find out exactly where in Khartoum this prison is situated," Holly said.

"I don't think it is in Khartoum," I said.

"Are you saying your informant gave you the wrong information?"

"Yes, but not deliberately. I think he thought that was the truth."

"So, Kayembe may not even be in Sudan."

I shrugged my shoulders. "Maybe. Maybe not. If we can find the prison, then maybe we will find him."

"I know a man—" Knocker started.

My eyes rolled. "You always know someone."

"What can I say? I'm well-traveled."

Holly said, "Reach out to him, Raymond. See what you can find out."

"Yes, ma'am."

Knocker made contact with his friend and got some information. It was like breaking a cipher code and nutting out every tenth word. When he came back to us a couple of days later, he said, "My friend says that the Russians have a big presence in Sudan. Training their military and stuff like that. Also, the politicians are using Russian mercs as bodyguards, and they are backing up police units to crack down on protests."

"But nothing about the prison?" I asked.

"No. But he said if anyone knows, it will be Faheem," Knocker said.

"Who is Faheem?"

"Local businessman. Works both sides of the fence."

I shook my head. "So, in other words, the guy is a criminal."

"Pretty much. If we see him and go from there."

"Shit." I looked at Holly. "Any news on Noskov?"

"Nothing has popped yet."

"Except for Reaper," Knocker said.

Frowning, I gave him my best WTF look. Then the penny dropped. "Idiot."

Holly sighed. "Give me a day and I'll get us into Khartoum. Small team. You two, me, and a couple of backups."

"Are you sure you can do it?" I asked.

"Leave it with me. I'll get it done."

Then something strange happened. My phone rang. The

number was blocked, and normally I wouldn't have answered, but something was telling me I needed to. "Yeah?"

"Hello, Mr. Kane."

The accent was unmistakable. "You have me at a disadvantage," I replied.

"Come now, Mr. Kane, I think you know who it is."

"Shatov?"

"Well done. I thought I should introduce myself to the man who has caused me no end of troubles."

Knocker and Holly just stared at me. "You're a hard man to track down."

Shatov chuckled. "And you are very hard to kill. Very persistent."

"I try."

"I don't suppose if I asked you nicely you would stop?"

"Not likely," I replied.

"I did not think so." He sighed and then said, "Oh, well, I guess we have nothing else to talk about."

"You could tell me where you are and we could visit. Shoot the shit, then I could kill you."

"You are a funny man."

"Or you could tell me what you're up to. You know, new oil field, diamonds."

"Whatever we are doing, it is too late to stop it, Mr. Kane."

"I can try."

"And you will die."

The line went dead. "Bye."

"What the fuck was that all about?"

"No idea."

"More to the point, how the hell did he get your number?" Holly asked. "I'll see if I can get someone to trace it."

"Don't bother. They're too good for that. How do you

think they've lived in the shadows for so long? No, we make Noskov our target."

"Fine, let's get ready to go to Khartoum."

After Holly left the room, Knocker came over to me. "Reaper, these pricks worry me. They seem to be able to do anything at will. And they know what we're doing before we do it."

"Yeah," I agreed. "All we can do is dismantle them a piece at a time."

"Fuck it."

CHAPTER 12

YOU ONLY WENT TO KHARTOUM IF YOU HAD TO. THEN YOU would be told to reconsider. The country was in a volatile state with factions fighting each other for control. It seemed that almost every corner had policemen or soldiers on it with mercenary escorts. Knocker had been here on an op some ten years before, looking for a terrorist known as Ramh or Spear. They had located him just outside the city in a compound surrounded by followers he was grooming to be suicide bombers. A drone strike had stopped his and their careers in an instant.

But we weren't here to find terrorists. We were here to find a man named Faheem. Intel had him working out of a café overseeing prostitutes. Word was that he made good money out of it and split it with the police, who permitted him to operate. That was out in the open. On the side, he provided a pipeline for illegal ivory that was shipped from the coast at Port Sudan.

The café we were looking for was on a quiet side street with nothing but hard-packed dirt for a base. We were driving a small Toyota van which had rust and bullet holes in it. When in Rome, you needed to blend it.

For a change, I drove while Knocker gave me directions. Our first hiccup came when I turned a corner, finding ourselves staring at a roadblock manned by police. We had passports, and once again, we were posing as press.

The van rolled to a stop just short of the roadblock. Our windows were down, allowing the heat and stink of this part of the city to blow through. There were four men on the roadblock armed with a mix of AK-47s and Chinese Type 56 assault rifles.

One of the soldiers approached my side while another walked up to Knocker's. Our handguns were hidden but within reach. The policeman on my side said something I couldn't understand. I said, "I don't understand."

He stared at me and said in halting English, "Who are you?"

I held up my press ID. "Press."

He looked at it, then at me, then at Knocker. "What about him?"

"Photographer. Takes pictures. Photos."

Knocker held up his camera and took a picture of the man. Then he showed him the photo on the back screen. "There you go, mate. See?"

He grunted. "What are you doing here?"

"Doing a report on the unrest."

Again, he grunted. "It's not safe for you. You should go back to your country."

"We are," I replied. "Just as soon as we get our story done."

The policeman grunted a final time and stepped back before waving us through. I engaged the van back into gear with a grating sound and gave it some gas. It coughed and wheezed then pulled forward, gathering speed. I said to Knocker, "You take shit photos."

"Why?" He sounded indignant.

"You cut his fucking head off."

He looked down at the screen. "Will you look at that. I did too."

"Wanker."

We found the café we were looking for five minutes later. It had a sandstone front and signage with faded and peeling paint above the door. There were three tables out front with two men and four women seated at them.

We parked the van and climbed out, hiding our weapons on us. As we approached the door, one of the women smiled at us, her white teeth stark against her almost ebony skin. "Hello, baby."

I kept walking. We passed inside through a beaded curtain. On the other side of the thin barrier, the strong scent of cigars assailed our senses. The café was dim and there were more girls inside. A man came up and greeted us. "If you are here for the girls, you pay upfront and you take them wherever. There are no rooms here for you to have sex."

"We're not here for the girls," I replied.

He held up a hand. "Not for men either. It is illegal in Sudan for you to do that."

"We're here to see Faheem."

"There is no one here by that name?"

"Are you sure?" asked Knocker as he peered at the table in the back of the café. "Who's that sitting at the table down there?"

"Customers."

I said, "Tell him we have ten thousand American dollars for him if he can help us out."

The man glanced at the table. A fly buzzed in the room, filling the void of silence. Our gazes followed the man's as we waited for something to happen. Then slowly, almost torturously, a large round man rose from the chair he'd been sitting on.

He crossed the floor toward us. Morbidly obese, the man reminded me of Jabba the Hutt.

"Who is this ugly motherfucker?" Knocker said softly. "I can feel the earth tremble every time he takes a fucking step."

"Shut up, will you," I hissed back at him.

"Gentlemen," the giant said. "I am Faheem. How can I help you?"

His voice boomed like James Earl Jones's had done and I was drawn more to the Star Wars analogy. "We came here to talk to you. A friend of ours said you would be the man who would know."

"What are your names?"

"Tom and Jerry," I replied.

Faheem chuckled. "You don't look much like a cat and a mouse."

I remained silent.

He stared at us some more before nodding. "Come, sit. Tell me what is worth ten thousand American dollars."

We followed him back to the table. He spoke to the two men and the two women already seated there and they gathered their things and got up and left. We sat down and Faheem asked, "Would you like coffee?"

"Sure, why not?"

A couple of minutes later the coffee was there. I took a sip. It was hot, strong, and bitter. Overall, it tasted like an elephant had shit in it. Faheem drank some of his and said, "Now, let's talk."

I reached inside my shirt and took out two bricks of money. I placed them in the middle of the table and saw the big man ogle them with greedy eyes. "That is yours if you help us out."

He reached his hand forward, but I pulled the bricks back. "But, if you lie to us, I'll make sure a fucking Hellfire missile lands on your fucking head and caves the bastard in."

He glared at me. "Speak respectfully."

"Just making sure we're on the same page."

He grunted. "I think we understand each other."

"Good. Ever heard of a place called Perdition?" I asked him.

"Maybe."

"It's a prison. Most likely run by the Russians."

"I might have heard of it," Faheem replied.

"Where is it?"

"In the desert."

"Can you show us where?" I asked.

"Do you have a map?"

Knocker reached into his shirt and retrieved one. He unfolded it and placed it on the table in front of us. Faheem leaned forward, his eyes roaming over the creased piece of paper.

His fat finger gently touched the map. "There."

"Middle of the desert," Knocker said. "Miles away from fucking anywhere."

"How do you know it's there?" I asked Faheem.

"I have girls. They hear things."

I pushed the money over in front of him. "How do we get inside?"

The big man grinned. "That, my crazy friend, is up to you."

We left after that and went back to the building on the outskirts where Holly and the two techs were holed up. "What did you find out?"

I showed her the map. "There."

"Middle of nowhere."

"That's right. Our main problem will be getting in there. We need photos of the place."

Holly nodded. "I'll get you some."

"Also, to assault a place like this, we're going to need backup," I informed her. "Can you get us a team of operators?"

"I might be able to pull a rabbit out of a hat for you. Let me make a few calls."

Holly made her calls and we waited. We couldn't plan anything without knowing what we were looking at. But that was only half the problem. We could see what was on the outside, but had no idea what things were like on the inside.

We needed to know.

———

The following day, we got the first look at our target. It appeared to be an old sandstone fort in the middle of nowhere surrounded by sand and rock and what looked to be an old riverbed that ran past it.

"Do we know what it is?" I asked Holly.

She nodded. "Fortress Dabala. It means Fortress Strong."

"What language?" I asked.

"It is a modern Nubian dialect."

Knocker and I looked at the pictures. The fort perimeter was loaded with crenellations with turrets at each corner which made it look like an old castle. The main gateway was arched and looked to be around fifteen feet at its highest point. There were buildings on the inside that looked like blockhouses and a parade ground. We could just make out figures on the ground and some trucks.

Knocker sighed. "Great, we have to take a bloody fortress to rescue one man."

"It's going to take at least two teams," I said.

"Yes, and then some. We'll need ropes, ascenders, helicopters on station. Maybe once everything goes down they could come in and fly cover."

I nodded. "If they can do that, we'll need strobes."

"I'll start making a list," Knocker said.

We ran through what we would need and soon we were done. I stared at the photos and said, "We're still missing something."

"What's that, Reaper?"

"We don't know what's inside."

"Thinking about calling for help?"

"Yes."

It was old friend time. I dug into my pocket for my cell and dialed a number which rang twice before being answered. "Reaper, this can't be good."

"Hey, Slick," I said. "I need your help."

Sam *Slick* Swift was a man Knocker and I had worked with in the past. He was someone who could find something when there was nothing there to find. He was, as they say, next level. "Lay it on me."

"Ever heard of Fortress Dabala?"

"Let me see. Hmm, Sudan? That the one?" he asked.

"That's it."

"Give me a minute—whoa, am I seeing what I think I am?"

"If what you're seeing is a bunch of armed guys on the ground, then yes."

"Are they Russian?" he asked.

"What are you looking at, Slick?"

"Satellite feed from a Chinese bird flying over the area as we speak."

This was just the type of thing he could do. And do it well. "The Russians call it Perdition," I told him.

"Shit, then it's true?"

"Looks that way," I replied. "I have a tough one for you."

"You make it sound like a challenge, Reaper. Are you going to talk dirty to me?"

"Yeah. I need to know what is on the inside. If I'm going in there, I need to know what to expect."

"How soon?"

"Yesterday."

"You'll have it. Great talking to you, Reaper."

"You too, Slick."

I disconnected the call and Knocker asked, "What do we do now?"

"I guess we wait."

Suddenly Holly appeared. "Get your stuff together. Someone just blew the shit out of Faheem. Looks like it was a drone strike."

"The generals?"

"Who knows, it could have been the Americans for all we know."

Knocker gave a false shiver. "Man, that would have left a fucking mess."

"Oh, yes."

We got our stuff and got the hell out of Dodge, as they say. We finished up across the road in Saudi Arabia. Not my first port of choice because Knocker and I weren't well-liked there. I guess we'd ruffled a few feathers there over the years.

"Was it the generals who killed Faheem?" German asked.

Holly shook her head. "We found out later that it was the Americans. Faheem wasn't just dealing in prostitution. He was also kidnapping girls off the street and shipping them to various terror organizations throughout Africa. He made Nigeria look like a holiday."

"You had no idea what was happening?" Christine Ryan asked.

"The Americans don't tell us much, ma'am. Unless it directly affects them or they want our help. We're pretty much the same."

"Yes, I'm afraid it has always been that way. Continue, Mr. Kane."

A few days later, we were ready to go.

Swift got back to us first with the layout of the fortress. He sent us all he'd dug up and gave us special interest with a couple of features. "See that, Reaper. That's a pipe. It is an old sewer outlet dating back maybe two hundred years. It obviously isn't working at the moment, but I think you should be able to use it to get in."

"What else do you have, Slick?"

He went through the other details including the cells which were below ground. "They're the old dungeons. I've marked how you can access them. It looks as though you'll need to secure the towers before you do much of anything."

"Yeah, we figured that."

"Reaper, I know you know what you're doing, but I've been around like you long enough to know this will not be an easy nut to crack."

"Yeah, I know. Thanks for your help, Slick."

"Anytime, Reaper. Just call."

The conversation ended and my friend was gone. At least we had an idea of what we were facing and what we needed to do.

The next to arrive was a team of SBS chaps. Sixteen men we would break up into a team of twelve and another of four. We went over the plan we would use for entry. I would take a team in through the tunnel and come up in the center of the fortress. Knocker and the SBS commander, Jack Rice, would go over the walls and secure the parapets. From there, the first team would go down to the dungeons to find the prisoner. The rest would stay above ground and deal with any threats that presented. From there we would call the two attack helicopters in. The transport would be the last in for extraction. It was a Merlin HM1.

I looked at Rice and said, "This is going to be hairy. I won't sugarcoat it."

"My lads are up to it," he reassured me.

"A school of flounder in the desert," Knocker jibed. "Wonderful."

Rice glanced at him and grinned. "Fuck off."

"I guess we're ready to go," I said.

Knocker nodded. "About time. I was getting bored drinking beer."

"Poor shite," Rice said.

———————

We were inserted by helicopter five kilometers from our target. Noise travels a long way over the desert, and we figured that where we put down behind the ridge would be reasonably safe. From there, we humped to the target. And we humped hard until we topped a low ridge and there it was, a sentinel standing in the desert darkness.

All of us were wearing the white phosphorus NODs and were packing extra ammo along with fragmentation and stun grenades. Two of the SBS chaps were packing DMRs—Designated Marksman Rifles. The rest of us were armed with C8s—L119A1 CQB Carbines.

I crouched down, and Knocker and Rice joined me. There were few lights on, but we knew from the photos that there were searchlights on each tower. Part of the reason we needed to capture the towers was to disable those.

"Why not disable the power system?" German asked.

"At that stage we weren't sure where it was—we had a fair idea—but if we did that, it would draw attention straight away."

He nodded. "Okay."

I said to Knocker and Rice, "You're all squared away with what you have to do?"

"Roger that," Rice said.

"Times two," replied Knocker.

"I'll let you know when we're in position."

I waved my team forward. Four men came to their feet. Lofty, Ginger, Henry, and Fuck Eyes. The military is a wonderful world of colorful handles for operators. We slipped down the slope toward the fort until we reached the dry riverbed and, using it for cover, circled to the right.

Ten minutes later, we reached the old sewer opening. It was constructed of sandstone blocks and bricks. Crouching there, I whispered into my comms, "Ghost One to Two and Three, copy?"

I got replies from both my team leaders. I said, "One is at Jericho. Going in now. Good luck."

We entered the ancient sewer. Ginger was on point. I was following him. The floor of the sewer had lifted and buckled over time. We moved cautiously, mindful of the chance the Russians had placed tripwires or motion sensors anywhere inside. As luck would have it, it was clear.

We eventually reached an exit point. A grate which was in the parade ground. I tapped Eyes and he handed his primary weapon to Henry. Then he started up the vertical opening which was just wider than a man. He used his feet and hands to put pressure on the walls and pull himself up. When he reached the grate, he wriggled it until it came free.

"Ghost Two and Three, One is at Carthage, over."

"Roger that. Two and Three are Charlie Mike."

There was no going back now.

———

Knocker and Rice went into action. The grappling hooks they were using were sent over the walls with a dull thud and locked in place. One by one, they hooked up their automatic ascenders and went up the wall. Knocker and Rice went first.

Once they were up, they paused on the parapet, momentarily taking in their immediate surrounding. All looked to be quiet. The two snipers took up their positions, concentrating on the far two towers where the sentries were.

Knocker took his team left and Rice right. They used the shadows as best they could, but the towers were open, not enclosed, so the risk of getting close without being seen was high. Both teams stopped short of their objectives. Knocker said in a low voice, "Three...two...one...execute."

Four men fired simultaneously. Knocker, Rice, and the two snipers. With those four shots, four men died. "Secure the towers and disable the lights."

A soldier appeared in the courtyard near the grate that our team was going to use. An operator near Knocker saw him come and put him down with two shots from his suppressed C8.

The two teams secured the towers and killed the searchlights. Then Knocker said over the comms, "Ghost One, perimeter secure."

"Roger that, coming on deck."

CHAPTER 13

Eyes cleared the grate and dropped the rope down to us in the sewer. Once it was secured, we used our ascenders and rose to the surface. When we were all up, we headed for the dungeon cells.

The entrance to the cell block looked like an old outhouse standing on its own. The door was locked. We had no hope of picking it because it was an old iron thing that you needed a proper key for. "Breacher up," I whispered.

Lofty came forward and set his charges. While he did this, I called in the helicopters. "Striker One-One, copy?"

"Copy, Ghost One."

"We're about to go loud. Bring your birds in. Out."

"One-One is inbound."

We pulled back from the door, and I touched Lofty on the shoulder. He said, "Breaching!" Then he detonated.

Ginger was the first man up. He reached the top of the stairs and threw a flashbang down. He pulled back and, once it had exploded, went down the steps. I heard him fire his weapon and say, "Contact front. X-ray down."

I was behind him on the old stone steps. When we hit

the bottom, everything opened out into a maze of hallways. Up top, the fortress may have looked the same, but below, it had been reconfigured.

A guard appeared in front of me, and I put him down with three rounds to the chest. I could hear the others firing their weapons, and after a few moments, the calls of 'clear!' were coming over the comms. Eventually, mine was one of them.

Then we set about finding our HVT.

Above ground, Knocker and the two teams were starting to become heavily engaged with the on-site force. Russian soldiers were coming out of the woodwork. Knocker fired a burst of gunfire toward a Russian soldier who was trying to pick off a target on the parapet. The man jerked and spasmed and fell onto his back.

Suddenly a light machine gun opened up right at the parapet where they were standing. Knocker threw himself down. "Ghost Three, can you get that bastard? I'm pinned down."

"Roger that, Ghost Two."

The SBS man opened fire, but his rounds fell short and the Russian kept firing his LMG. "Son of a bitch."

Rice said into his comms, "Johnno, get that bastard."

The second of the two snipers realigned his rifle and picked out the LMG operator. He centered the crosshairs on the man's head and fired a shot. Johnno saw the man's head snap back as a bullet punched into his brain. "X-ray down."

Overhead, one of the helicopters came in and snipers in the doorway started opening fire, covering the ground force. Knocker and the other operators held the high ground, but they were still taking heavy fire from the numerous Russians below. He reached for a fragmentation grenade, pulled the pin, and threw it near a truck where four Russians were hiding. The explosion was instant. The truck went up, engulfing the four Russian shooters who were there beside it. They staggered free, each of them burning, their clothes on fire. The screams were high-pitched. A couple of SBS men opened fire at them and put them all down in a tight, compact area.

Someone shouted, "RPG!"

Overhead, the helicopter did another lazy circuit of the Fort. Knocker said into his comms, "Everyone make sure that their strobes are on. I don't want them getting shot from the helicopter by mistake."

Rice appeared at Knocker's side. "We need to clear them out from down there so we can push forward."

"I agree. Tell your boys to keep their heads down."

"Roger that."

"Striker One-One, copy?"

"Copy, Ghost Two."

"I need your boy to rake the parade ground with his minigun, over."

"Copy, Ghost Two."

Suddenly, the minigun on the helicopter opened up. The parade ground turned into a blazing hell as minigun rounds hammered into it. They didn't discriminate. They ripped through flesh and metal and earth without hesitation. Empty cases rained down from above like a cloud had opened and released them.

Knocker heard the screams from the wounded and dying. The helicopter pulled away and started to do another lazy circuit. Knocker said into his comms, "Team One and Team Two, move down into the parade ground."

The SBS men pressed forward. They ran down the

closest stairs to their position and onto the hard-packed earth below. A Russian shooter appeared and an SPS operator put a bullet through the man's head with his handgun.

"Rice, secure this area," Knocker said.

"Copy that."

"My team, follow me."

Knocker ran toward a large building. The door was locked, and he took a step to the side. "Breacher up."

A soldier appeared and placed the breaching charge on the door. He stepped sideways out of the blast zone, looking to Knocker for his order.

The former SAS man said, "Do it."

The breaching charge detonated with a loud roar. Knocker stepped forward into the dust cloud, ready to clear the room beyond. A figure appeared and fired at the former SAS man. Bullets cracked past his head, and Knocker fired his own weapon. The shooter cried out in pain and fell to the floor. Knocker took a step forward and shot him again to make sure.

Glancing around the room, Knocker saw the radios and telephones. It was a communication room. There were computers as well.

Turning to the man next to him, Knocker said, "Get everything you can."

"Roger that, boss."

"Right. The rest of you guys, follow me. Let's clear this fucking place out."

———

Down below in the dungeons, we were clearing the prison cells one at a time. Some of them were occupied. By whom, I don't know, but we left the doors open and let them go. It wasn't until I had tried the 4th cell that I found who we were looking for.

"President Kayembe?" I asked.

The haggard-looking man nodded. "I am he."

"We're here to get you out, sir. You need to come with us and do everything exactly as we tell to you."

"Who are you?"

"Just call us your friends, sir."

I helped him out of the cell. He was limping. I said into my comms, "Ginger, on me."

"Coming, boss."

A few moments later, Ginger appeared. I said to him, "Look after the president. Guard, the man with your life."

"You got it, boss."

We started back toward the stairs. I went up first, followed by Lofty. Ginger and the president followed him with Henry, and Fuck Eyes was bringing up the rear. I paused at the top. Not wanting to walk out into a hail-storm of bullets. "This is Ghost One to all call signs. I say again, Ghost One to all call signs. We have the president. We're coming out. Do us a favor and don't fucking shoot us."

I opened the door immediately, and a round cracked into the side of the jamb near my head. I brought up my C8 and trained on to the shooter I could just make out near a vehicle. I stroked the trigger and the weapon fired. The Russian jerked as rounds hammered into him. He staggered and then fell to the hard-packed earth. I turned to Ginger and said, "Get him out of here."

Lofty and I provided cover fire as Ginger half-carried the president toward our RV. We then ran over to another truck and crouched down beside it, using the engine block for cover. "This is Ghost One to all call signs. Time to go. Striker One-One, copy?"

"Copy, Ghost One."

"I need you to provide covering fire as we withdraw."

"Roger that."

I still had one more call to make. "Carrier Two-Four, copy?"

"Copy, Ghost One."

"Two-Four, we—"

Bullets punched into the truck, interrupting my call. I tried again. "Two-Four, we need immediate extract, over."

"Copy, Ghost One, Two-Four is inbound."

"Knocker, where are you?"

"On my way out. We have a shitload of goodies."

"Don't take too long. The chopper's inbound."

"Will be right on your ass."

"Copy. All call signs, withdraw now. The helicopter is on the way in. Meet at the RV."

We all climbed the steps up to the parapet and found the ropes that had been used for the infiltration of the fortress. We rappelled down them, and once we were all gathered at the base, we headed out into the desert to meet the helicopter. Meanwhile, the other strike helicopters were covering us from above.

By the time we reached the LZ, the helicopter was coming in. Knocker and his people had caught up, and by some miracle, the only casualty we had was an SBS soldier with a blister on his heel caused by new boots.

A few minutes later, we'd loaded Kayembe and us onto the helicopter and had lifted off. I sat next to Knocker, and we bumped fists. We knew we'd been lucky.

———

"What about the intelligence you scraped together?" German asked. *"What became of that?"*

"It was all handed over to MI6," Holly said.

"What was in it?"

"Most of it was about the other prisons. They were able to use it to locate them and order simultaneous raids to

extract prisoners who were determined to be of certain value."

"Was there anything else? About the generals, maybe?"

"No," I said. "Nothing about them at all."

"Very well, take another break and we'll reconvene in thirty minutes, and you can move on to Belgium."

We left the conference room and went back to the canteen for coffee. "How do you think it's going?" Knocker asked Holly.

She shrugged. "It could be going well, and they would decide to lock us all up."

I sipped my coffee. Holly said, "They're going to want to know about Short."

"Let them ask," Knocker said. "I'll tell them what happened."

"That might not be wise," Holly said.

"No, he's right. We just stick to the truth."

"Okay," Holly replied.

We drank our coffee and went over things that were still to come. Once we were done, we sat and talked more until a security officer came to retrieve us. Back in the conference room, we took our all-too-familiar seats. Christine Ryan frowned at us like we were school-children late for class. "You are late."

"We were smoking cigarettes behind the shed," Knocker replied.

I grinned. It was funny, even if they didn't think so. German sighed. "All right, let's move on. I'm really looking forward to this part. Another example of a couple of out-of-control neanderthals."

Knocker frowned. "Reaper, did he just call us cavemen?"

"I do believe he did."

He nodded in satisfaction. "Good, I was worried he was going to call us smart."

"Why would that worry you?" I asked.

"Because I've met a few smart people lately." He stared at German. "And they're all fucking dumb."

German lurched to his feet. "Why, you—"

"Sit down, cunt, before I put you through the wall behind you," Knocker growled.

"All right, enough," Christine Ryan snapped. *"Maybe we should adjourn until tomorrow. When everyone has cooled down."*

I shook my head. "No, we do this now. Tomorrow we'll have other things to discuss."

"Okay, Mr. Kane. Let's continue before your friend and my colleague insult each other to death."

We got off the plane at RAF Brize Norton and were met by Short and his driver. "How were things?"

"They went well for once," Holly told him. "Surprisingly."

"What makes you say that?" he asked, turning in his seat to look at us.

"Because these people seem to always be one step ahead of us."

Short nodded. "Yes, I was thinking about that. Do you think there could be a leak?"

"A mole?" Holly clarified.

"Yes."

She looked at Knocker and me. "I suppose it's possible."

"I'll put someone onto it. Now, well done on the Kayembe job. The boss said to pass on his congratulations on a job well done."

"Job's only half done," I said to him.

Short nodded. "Yes, well, you're being stood down for a while. You've been working hard for some time, so you should appreciate the rest."

He was right. We needed the break. We'd been running and gunning for a while and we needed to recharge. "I'm not going to argue with you."

"Good. We'll tidy up the paperwork and then you are all free to go."

So, that's what we did. We finished our paperwork and went our own separate ways for a few days. I spent the first night in a hotel, not wanting to bring my troubles upon anyone close to me. Knocker went to Kent, found a pub, and got drunk. Holly was with me that first night. After that, she went to Crantock in Cornwall.

The day she left, I spent the rest of it in front of the television, catching up on what was happening in the world. Sergey Lash was playing hardball. He was holding rallies for the public, stating that Russia would be great again in the eyes of the West. It would be a world superpower to behold.

Meanwhile, in the DRC, Elia had announced all hostilities had ceased and his country was calming down. The UN was vowing to investigate war crimes that had occurred in the country, but I knew they wouldn't get far.

That night I ordered Chinese takeout and ate it in my room, washed down by beer. Then I watched a couple of John Wayne westerns on a movie channel.

My cell rang. "Yeah?"

"Enjoying your break, Mr. Kane?"

"Shatov?"

"Who else?"

"To answer your question, I was. Not so much now."

"A shame. I just rang to congratulate you on a wonderful effort to rescue Mr. Kayembe."

"I don't get it. You and your cronies spend decades in the dark, and yet this is the second time you've called me."

"I guess it doesn't matter where I am concerned. You already know who I am. And General Noskov."

He knew that we knew Noskov's name. "How about you tell me what you're up to and fill in that blank."

He chuckled. "Even if I did, you still couldn't stop it. No, I'll let you figure that one out for yourself."

"I'll get there."

"By the way, how is your family—or should I say, sister?"

My blood ran cold at the mention of Melanie. "If you think you can get to her, think again, Shatov. The people at Global won't let anyone within a thousand yards of her."

"Very true," he replied.

Had the son of a bitch already tried?

He sensed my concern and said, "They are very good."

"Fuck you."

"Now, now, no need to be uncivil."

"I will get you, Shatov."

"I'm sure you will try, Mr. Kane. Anyway, I must go. And as you westerners say, toodles."

The call disconnected and he was gone.

I dialed a number. "Hi, John."

Melanie's voice relaxed me instantly. I said, "How's things, Mel?"

"Good…if you like being held prisoner."

"I know, I'm sorry."

"It's not that bad, John. I know why I'm here. Cara is great, and so is Mary. I even get an armed escort if I go somewhere. Even to the store."

Relief flooded through me. We talked some more and said goodbye. "Please be careful, John."

"I'll be fine. I've got Knocker."

"That's what worries me. By the way, don't forget my birthday."

Shit. "I won't."

I made one more call after Mel. "Hey, Holly."

"John? What's up?"

"Shatov called."

"We'll have to change your cell out."

"No, let him call. This way, he might keep slipping up."

"Keep slipping up?"

"He knows we know Noskov's name."

"Blast. When we get back, we need to figure out our next move."

"Finding Noskov," I replied.

"He'll go to ground."

"Yes, most likely. But we could try to find a way to draw him out."

"I'll think about it. You do it too. Maybe together we can figure something out."

————

I was right. Noskov met with Shatov, who ordered him to be more discreet. "I'm sorry, Mikhail, it was careless of me."

"Do not worry, Lazar, they know who I am." Shatov looked around the table. "I'm grateful the remainder of you remain relatively unscathed."

One of them cleared his throat.

Shatov nodded in acknowledgment. "Sorry. I was forgetting about you. However, I would like you to go to Antwerp and visit our diamond buyer. Prepare them for a bigger shipment."

The general nodded. "I can do that, sir."

"We want them converted over to bearer bonds like the last lot. I'm told that there should be almost a billion dollars. Am I correct?"

"Yes, sir."

"Good, now how is production coming along?"

"One of the mines has hit a rich pocket. Best estimates say that it could produce a further three billion dollars."

Shatov was surprised. It was a wonderful windfall. Most mines struggled to produce a third of that per year. "It looks like things are proceeding ahead of schedule."

"Yes, sir."

Shatov ran his gaze over the men at the table. They were loyal men, devoted to the cause. So far, in spite of the hiccups, everything was on track. And God willing, they would succeed.

————

The following day, I found myself using my time to find something for Mel's birthday. Hatton Garden had an abundance of jewelers so that was where I was. I thought maybe a necklace with an angel on it. I wasn't sure of gold or silver. Besides, if she didn't like it, she could exchange it.

I visited three stores and came up empty. The fourth provided fruit. An angel on a chain. White gold and a diamond in each of her wings. I looked at the young lady behind the counter. "How much are we talking?"

She looked at the price tag. "Three thousand pounds."

"Do you accept blood?"

She gave me a weird look. I reached into my pocket and took out my wallet. I was about to pay when two armed men wearing ski masks burst in. One also held a hammer. He pointed at me with his sawn-off shotgun and yelled, "Back the fuck up or I'll kill you, motherfucker."

"Do you always attract trouble, Mr. Kane?" Christine Ryan asked me. "To me, it seems that you do."

"Let's just say that it would seem that I am the chosen person to solve the world's issues."

The young lady behind the counter paled, as did her assistant. The manager came from the back room and froze, his mouth agape. I thought the young woman who was serving me was about to faint. The man with the hammer started smashing the display cases while his accomplice started to fill the bag in his hand.

It was a dangerous situation and I'd decided that I would remain where I was and let them go. That was until two things happened. The guy with the shotgun snatched the necklace I had picked out for Mel's birthday from the young woman's hand and then slapped her for no reason.

I stared at him, and he caught me watching. "What the fuck are you looking at?"

"You didn't have to hit her," I said.

"Hey," his friend called. "Leave it. We have to go."

Shotgun man leaned in close. "I'll do whatever I fucking want. If you don't like it, then do something about it, mate."

His breath smelled of alcohol. Probably needed some courage to get the job done. I would guess he was drugged to the eyeballs on something too. Good for me, not for him. His reflexes would be slow. And they were.

I swept the shotgun aside and hit him in the throat. Immediately, he let the weapon go as he grabbed at his throat, gasping for air. I hit him again, this time in the face. He dropped like a stone, the hammer in his hand thumping to the floor.

His friend was stunned by the sudden developments and backed away from me. I took a few steps forward and said, "Pal, don't make me chase you. I'm not in the mood."

The shotgun centered on his chest. His hands flew so fast into the air I thought they would detach. "Don't shoot."

"You have a car outside?"

"Y-yes."

"Driver?"

"Yes?"

"He armed?"

"Yes."

"Are you armed?"

"No."

"Sit down," I snapped.

The robber did as he was ordered.

"If you move, I will shoot you."

I walked outside, the shotgun in my hands. I was holding onto the barrel when I swung it at the driver's side window. The window shattered under the force, spraying the driver with glass. Then I reached inside and dragged him out. Didn't worry about opening the door. I was too pissed. Once he was free, I dropped him on the street.

The driver looked up at me, confused. "What the fuck?"

Then I hit him. More than once. Anger in each blow.

Soon he was a bleeding heap on the street, and I was surrounded by onlookers.

But I wasn't done.

I grabbed the shotgun and went back inside. The robber who had hit the young woman was trying to get to his feet.

I hit him again.

And an idea came to me.

CHAPTER 14

"YOU JUST CAN'T STAY OUT OF TROUBLE, CAN YOU?" SHORT growled at me. "Send you on a break and you still manage to get involved in shit. Christ, the police wanted to throw the fucking book at you. I had to call in a favor from Five just to keep you out."

"I was buying a birthday present for my sister," I replied.

"Did you find her something nice, Reaper?" Knocker asked.

"I did, thank you."

"Oh, shut up, the pair of you." His gaze focused on Holly. "Do you have anything to say?"

"I was in Crantock," Holly replied.

"Windy down there?" Knocker asked.

"It was a bit."

"I hope it never ruined your—"

"Shut up!" We stood in silence. Short said, "I should send you all to the Falklands to count birds or whatever the bloody hell they do there. But you'd still get into trouble. So the question is, what do you think I should do with you?"

"Send us to rob a bank," I replied.

Holly leaned forward to look at me around Knocker. It

was her *are you fucking crazy* expression. Short, on the other hand, said, "For a moment, Mr. Kane, I thought you were joking, but then I realized that you are that crazy. I don't know why, but you have the floor."

"They have to be sending their diamonds somewhere," I elaborated. "It has to be Western Europe. The question is where? If we can find out, then we steal them. We steal their money, someone is going to come looking."

"Why not take them back to their own country?" Short asked.

Holly knew why. "Because they need them to be converted into some type of currency. I'm going to say bearer bonds. It's easier that way, and Russian banks still accept them."

Short nodded. "Find me something, Holly."

"Yes, sir."

We left his office and walked down the hallway. Knocker stopped and said, "Reaper, there is only one person I know of who can do this."

"Yeah, I'm with you. I'll make the call."

"Who?" Holly asked.

"Slick," Knocker replied.

———

I picked Slick up off the tube and took him back to HQ. Along the way, we discussed what was happening. He said, "Reaper, this sounds like child's play."

I was glad he was confident, but I still said, "Don't be so sure. These people, as you know, are dangerous. That and the fact they're one step ahead of us on most occasions. I need you to find me a leak."

"You have a leak?"

"I'm starting to feel like the poor bastard with his fingers in the dike."

"I'll see what I can do to relieve your tension," the redheaded tech said.

"One more thing. You carry at all times."

"Reaper, no—"

"You have no say in the matter, Slick. I'll find you something. I know you don't like weapons as such, but I know you can use them."

"Fine."

We arrived at HQ and Slick went right to work. He started by checking flights with pictures and companies and banks that dealt in diamonds. While he was doing that, he also had facial recognition running overtime in various countries. I swear, with all the equipment he had running, it was chewing power off the grid.

Three hours later, we had our first breakthrough. "Reaper, you should see this."

I moved around so I could see the screen. "What are we looking at?"

"Do you know this guy?"

I stared at the screen. "Noskov."

Slick nodded. "That was taken a week ago. He was leaving the Antwerp Diamond Exchange. He's carrying a briefcase."

"No prizes for guessing what's in there," I said.

"Has to be bearer bonds."

"Without a doubt."

"You say that was a week ago?" Holly asked.

"Yes."

"Can you find out where he went after that?"

"I can try. Like you said, these guys are good," Slick explained. "When he got out of the sedan, all the surveillance cameras around the precinct crashed. Except this one. Someone messed up."

"I know you have a but, Slick," I said.

He grinned. "We might be able to use this to our advantage."

"You mean the whole camera outage thing?"

"Yes, I can create a program to notify me every time something like this happens."

"Good. Do it."

Holly asked, "Are you coming?"

"Where?"

"To see Short. If we want to go to Antwerp, we need to convince him."

"Lead the way."

———

We found Short in his office. He looked up from reading intel reports and said, "By the looks on your faces, I'd say you might have something."

"We just picked up a frame of Noskov in Antwerp coming out of the diamond exchange," Holly told him.

"Can you confirm it is him?"

"I can," I replied. "I know what he looks like."

"So, you're here to tell me you want to go to Antwerp."

"Yes, sir."

"Find me more."

I frowned at him. "What do you mean more? Isn't that enough?"

"I want more."

"That's fine," Holly said. "We'll find you more."

We walked out of Short's office and Holly could tell I was angry. "John, leave it. We'll get more. Then we'll go."

"What damn more could he want? We've got one of the generals on site."

"Let it go. He wants more, we'll get it for him."

———

The following day, Slick found more. He had me come to him, and he showed me the camera feed from the Antwerp Palace, a five-star hotel in the center of the city. "I figure this was where he was staying, Reaper. Every so often, the cameras would glitch. Do you see it?"

At first, I saw nothing, then came the flicker. "Running on a loop?" I asked him.

"Almost, and partly, yes. It was only a minute, perhaps not even that. Every time it happened, it was only for a short period of time."

"Just long enough for someone to walk past and not be seen?" I asked.

Slick nodded. "Yes."

"When was this?"

"The same time Noskov was in Antwerp," he replied.

"Anything since?"

"No, which means he could be long gone."

"Is it time stamped?"

"Yes, as you can see."

"Can you alter it?"

Slick stared at me. "Why would I want to do that?"

"Because the only way we're going to get to Antwerp is for you to do it. We have to make Short think that Noskov is still there."

"You said we."

"Yes, you're coming too."

"I was afraid that was what you meant."

"Well?" I asked.

"Okay, I'll do it. But if anyone finds out, you've put a gun to my head."

I slapped him on the shoulder. "And pulled the trigger."

It took him not much time at all and once it was done, Slick downloaded the feed onto a drive and gave it to me. First, I gave it to Holly to look over with Knocker present.

As they watched it, I said, "The footage was taken the same day as Noskov went to the diamond exchange."

Holly stared at the screen and cocked her head to one side. "But this is time stamped yesterday."

"Yes, I had Slick alter it."

"Niice," Knocker grunted.

"Why would you do that?"

"To convince Short that we need to get to Antwerp," I explained. "We can't do anything here with our hands tied behind our backs."

"If he finds out…"

"Then we'd best make sure he doesn't."

Holly sighed resignedly. "Okay, let's go see him."

We caught Short in a hallway on his way out of the office to a meeting with an MP. He didn't say which one, and we didn't ask. When we told him we had something for him to see, he said he'd look at it later. "Just bring it to me when I get back."

"Yes, sir," Holly said.

"Actually, bring it to me first thing in the morning."

"Yes, sir."

Once he was out of earshot, I said, "Why didn't you push it?"

"There was no point, John. You and I both know that Noskov is more than likely gone from Antwerp. Get Swift to find something we can use when we get there."

"What do you mean?"

"Well, for starters, find out who he was dealing with there. Maybe how they are transporting the diamonds? If there is another shipment due? Stuff like that."

"Okay, I'll get him onto it."

"Thank you." She paused. "Remember, John, I'm on your side. I want to know what is happening just as much as you do. Until then, we have to keep digging."

"Yes, ma'am."

She glared at me. "Don't do that shit, either. We slept together, remember."

Holly stormed off along the hallway and left me standing there. Once she was gone, I turned around and went to see Slick.

———

"Do I need to pack my toothbrush?" he asked.

"Not yet." I told him what Holly wanted done. He nodded and said, "I'll see what I can dig up. Say, you don't want to split a pizza and a beer?"

"Did someone mention pizza and beer?" Knocker asked as he approached us.

I grinned. "You'd better make that order three pizzas and a six-pack."

———

It was early the following morning when Short came in to find Holly and me waiting for him. We showed him the feed, and he once again shook his head. "It could be just a glitch."

"Listen, if we don't act now, we could miss him. It is the perfect opportunity to get the bastard."

"And if he's not there?"

"We can gather intel about the diamonds and what they're doing with them."

"And what do you think they're doing with them?"

"Transferring them into bearer bonds and then converting them to money when they get back to Moscow."

Short thought about his response then said, "Fine. But I'm coming with you. I'll be in command of the operation. Is there a problem with that?"

Not what I was expecting, but… "Not in the slightest."

We flew to Antwerp on a Cessna Citation Sovereign jet. There were the five of us, plus the pilots. An apartment in the city was where we made our base. It had three rooms. Short got one, Holly got one, and we three—Knocker, Slick, and me—squeezed into the last one. We were there but a few minutes before Slick was online and working.

The rest of the apartment was open plan with a tiled floor. The dark drapes that hung across the glass sliding door hung all the way to the floor and were stiff and coarse. The balcony overlooked a narrow street that was busy with foot traffic.

I stood at the balcony rail and stared across the street at the other buildings. Most of the windows were doors and had balconies like the one I was on. Some of the drapes were drawn, some weren't. A lot of the buildings showed their age through cracks and their façade design.

I went back inside and saw Slick working hard. "You got anything?"

He gave me a look which made me nod. I turned away and found Knocker lying on the sofa with his feet up. "Didn't take you long."

"Sleep while you can, Reaper, you know that."

"Yeah, I also know we have places to be. Get up."

He swung his feet onto the floor. "Shit."

"Short, do you have the keys to the SUV?" I asked.

"What do you want them for?" he asked.

"Going to the hotel where we think Noskov is. Ask a few questions."

He tossed me the keys. "Don't destroy the place."

"I'll try not to."

We had hired a black Range Rover at the airport, and that was what Knocker and I used to get to the hotel where Noskov had stayed. We parked across the street from it, tucked our Glocks out of sight, and put our earwigs in before climbing out.

Knocker and I paused then jogged across the street and up onto the sidewalk.

Inside the foyer was a light travertine tile on the floor. They were large and rectangular in shape. Against the wall, there was a large marble statue of a woman, semi-clothed, a child at her feet. A chandelier hung from the ceiling, and the counter where the suited receptionist stood was a highly polished mahogany.

The man shook his head. "Can I help you, gentlemen?" he asked in Dutch.

I shook my head. "You speak English, friend?"

He nodded. "A little. Yes."

I took the photo out of my pocket and said, "Do you know if this man is still here?"

"I do not think so, sir. Even if he was, I could not tell you. It would be against our hotel policy."

It was to be expected, so my hand went into my coat pocket, and I produced a small wallet. I flicked it open and let him look at it. Knocker said, "Mate, we both work for Interpol. Now, unless you want him to arrest you for obstruction, I suggest you help."

The man gave an apologetic shrug. "I'm sorry. Unless you have a warrant, I cannot help you."

I'd expected as much and nodded. "Then we'll get one."

"Wait, Reaper, I'm not done. You have to stay there," Slick said hurriedly in my ear.

So, my stare never wavered, my eyes locked on the guy behind the desk as though it was a stare-down. I felt like a goose, and the counter guy was starting to look uncomfortable. He said, "Is that all?"

"Are you sure you can't help?"

"Sorry, sir."

I stared at him some more then Slick said, "Okay, got it."

I tapped the counter, turned, and walked out. "Shit, Slick, what the fuck?"

"There was some trouble getting onto the system from your cell. Got there eventually. I do have something interesting though."

"What's that?"

"I'll explain when you get back."

We climbed into the Range Rover, and Knocker started the vehicle and pulled away from the sidewalk. I saw him glance in the rearview mirror. "You saw it too, huh?"

He nodded. "Yeah. Two back, black sedan."

Looking into the side mirror, I picked it up. "Looks to be two in it. Just a tail I would say."

"And so it begins again," Knocker said, his voice dripping with sarcasm. "Slick, you still with us?"

"Hellooo, Raymond."

"Don't start that shit. We're having trouble with our comms. Can you reset them?"

"They seem to be fine from here," he replied.

"No, they're not, reset them."

"Okay."

A few moments later, he asked, "How is that?"

"Depends," Knocker replied.

"Good, all clear."

"Are you saying you're the only one who can hear us?"

"Yes, it mustn't have reset properly."

"We've got a tail. How are you with that leak?"

"I'll try again, Knocker," he replied.

"Black sedan."

"Roger that. I'll reset again now."

"Copy."

I looked at Knocker. "Subtle."

"I thought so."

We continued heading back to the apartment. Except when Knocker parked, he put the SUV about four buildings away. The black sedan parked back a ways, but Knocker wasn't done. Getting out of the SUV, he took out his Glock and walked back along the parked vehicles toward our tail.

Not wanting him to be lacking support, I did the same. Suddenly tires screeched and the sedan left its park and sped off along the street past us. I called over to Knocker, "Did you get a look?"

"No, the tint was too dark. But I'll tell you one thing, Reaper, I'm starting to get fucking pissed off."

"Yeah, me too."

CHAPTER 15

"WHAT DID YOU HAVE, SLICK?" I ASKED HIM WHEN WE GOT
back into the apartment.

"Not a what, Reaper, a who."

"All right."

A photo appeared of a woman going into the hotel
flanked by two men. She wore a knee-length coat, which
looked to be over a short black dress. She also had dark hair
and dark glasses. "That is Corry Van Beek."

"Who is Corry Van Beek?" I asked.

"Diamond buyer. She deals in black-market diamonds as
well as above-board stones. She also deals in bearer bonds."

"I'm guessing she was there to see Noskov."

Slick nodded. "You assume correct. Not long after she
arrived, the cameras glitched again."

"Shit. Were you able to get anything from what you
downloaded?"

"Still working on it."

"What about the other thing?" I asked.

"That might take a while."

"Work faster. Someone knows we're here because
they're already following us."

"I'm only one man, Reaper."

"Yes, sorry."

"What do you want me to prioritize?" Slick asked.

"The diamonds and Noskov and the other thing," I replied.

Slick rolled his eyes. "You're a hard man, Reaper."

"Better than being a dead one."

———

"Anything?" Holly asked as I stood on the balcony watching the street.

"Two things. A diamond buyer named Corry Van Beek, and we were followed."

"You were followed?" she seemed surprised.

I nodded. Looking back in through the glass of the door I saw Short sitting and working at a table. "How many people knew we were coming here?"

"Not many," Holly replied.

"The same people who have been with us from the outset?"

"Some, not all."

"How well do you know Short?"

"Brian?" Her excitement rose.

"Yes."

"Not too long. He was already in charge of the Middle East desk when I came in."

"Before that?"

"I don't know."

"Okay."

"I don't believe that it could be him."

"Well, it's not me or Knocker. Which leaves him, you, and whoever else was in the know."

"Now it's me?" Holly's tone had turned bitter.

"I didn't say that. Just that it was possible. Can you get

the names of those who know to Slick so he can do a deep dive on them?"

"Sure."

"Thanks, now, do you see that black sedan down there?"

"Yes."

"Our friends are back."

———

Knocker and I waited until dark before we acted. We took our Glocks and went down to the street, going out the back way so we could circle around the apartment block and through a narrow alley that was barely wide enough for a person to walk through.

We came out from behind the vehicle and walked toward it. There were two men inside. Both were so intent on what they were doing they weren't watching their six. I opened the rear door on the driver's side and climbed in, placing the muzzle of my Glock against the driver's head. Knocker did the same with the passenger. "Don't move, Comrade. Knocker, check them for weapons."

He leaned forward between the seats and relieved them of two handguns. The driver said, "You don't know what you are doing?"

His accent was French, not Russian. "Then talk. You've got two minutes before we put bullets in your heads and leave you here for the police to find."

"We are Interpol officers," the driver replied. "Pierre and Francois."

"ID?"

"In our coat pockets," Pierre replied.

Knocker leaned forward again and found what he was looking for. "He's telling the truth, Reaper."

Knocker gave their IDs back, but we held onto their weapons. I said, "Tell me why you were following us?"

"We received a tip about some diamond thieves in Antwerp who were about to perform a large robbery. We were given a file with your pictures in it."

"How did you know where we would be?"

"The address was in the file."

"Fucking bollocks," Knocker growled.

I said, "Gentlemen, come with us and we'll get this sorted out."

"What do you mean?"

"We're British Intelligence."

We took them inside and sat them down in the center of the room. Once the formalities were out of the way, I said, "Where did your intel come from?"

"I don't know. We got it from Lyon. It was sent through."

"How did they get it?" Short demanded. "No one was supposed to know we were here."

"I said I don't know," Pierre snapped.

"Why are you here?" Francois asked.

Everyone remained silent so I took the initiative and lied. Partly. "We're looking into diamonds. Most likely stolen. The people we're looking at are possibly terrorists and could be meeting a buyer."

Short and Holly both stared at me. Knocker didn't waver. Pierre said, "Who is the buyer?"

"Corry Van Beek."

"The seller?"

With a shake of my head, I said, "We don't know."

"Why is British Intelligence looking into stolen diamonds?" Francois asked.

"Like I said, it could have a terrorist angle."

"Does the Belgian government know you are here?"

"Do they know you're here?" I asked, taking a punt that they never did .

"I guess we are both in the same way."

"I guess we are. Do your people know much about Van Beek that we could use?" I asked him.

"Maybe some. What do you want to know?"

"Like where she resides?"

"Paris."

"Do you know if she is there now?"

"No, she is in Antwerp. She arrived yesterday."

"How about where she is staying in Antwerp?" I asked.

"She has a villa outside the city. She stays there under close guard."

"I'll need an address."

Pierre wrote one down and handed it over.

"Thanks for your help," I said and gave them back their weapons.

"Maybe once you have something, you can pass the information on," Pierre said.

"Sure," I lied. Then they left.

"What the hell was that?" Short demanded.

"Don't you mean how the fuck did they know we were here?" Knocker corrected him.

"Of course."

"Then find the hell out, Short. Make yourself fucking useful."

"You can't speak to me like that," he snapped indignantly.

"Whatever."

"Slick, did you track that address?"

"Got it, Reaper."

"She's obviously in town for another buy. We need to find out where and when."

"And who," Holly said.

It was getting close to midnight when Slick came to me. I was lying on my bed, Knocker on the single beside me. "Reaper, you awake?"

"Yeah."

"I have something."

I turned the lamp on beside the bed. Knocker rolled away from the brightness. He said, "If it's not a hand grenade, I don't want to fucking know."

"What is it, Slick?"

"I picked out a name that fits the timeline of when Noskov was here. Kozlov. First name Igor."

"Common name," I replied.

"Yes, it is. He paid by card, and it traced back to a tractor manufacturing company in Moscow. I looked into it and found it to be a shell corporation."

"So, that could have been Noskov."

"Sure. But while I was looking through, I came up with something else. Another name linked to the same company. Alexey Sokolov."

"Arrival?"

"The day after tomorrow."

"All right, that gives us a bit over twenty-four hours to check on Van Beek."

"That's not going to be as easy as you think," Slick said. "She was former Belgian army. Rank of Major before she was kicked out."

"Why was she kicked out?" Knocker asked, his voice muffled against the pillow.

"She got caught bringing diamonds into Belgium. It wasn't the first time she'd done it because she had a secret bank account with a couple of million dollars in it. She also had a raft of safety deposit boxes across Antwerp. After she got kicked out, she moved to Paris but stayed in the rock business."

"Illegal and legal."

Slick nodded. "That's about it."

"What about Short?" I asked Slick.

"That's a strange one. He used to be Berlin Station boss before being dragged back to London after twelve months and put on the Middle East desk."

"Punishment?"

"Could be, I'm not sure."

"Berlin is a top gig," Knocker said. "For him to be dragged back to London after twelve months, he must have pissed someone off. Does it say who issued the order?"

"Someone called Christine Ryan."

"Anything you would like to add on the subject?" I asked her.

She shook her head. "Not particularly."

"How about why you called him back? It might fill in a few holes."

"Maybe you don't need to know?"

"Did you know what the op was he was running at the time?"

"No."

"Okay, Slick, find out what you can."

The computer tech left our room and I sat up, swinging my legs over the side of the bed. Knocker took a quick glance and buried his head. I heard a muffled, "Fucking hell."

"Get up, Raymond. We've got work to do."

We got out of bed and dressed. Grabbed our Glocks and I went into Holly's room and woke her. "What is it?" she asked, still half asleep, her voice low and husky.

"Knocker and I are going out."

"Where?"

"Surveillance on Corry Van Beek."

"All right, but keep in touch."

"Roger that."

———

The villa, as we'd been told, was on the outskirts of Antwerp. We were able to watch it from the seclusion of a wood on a low hill to its west, which afforded us a clear view of its entrance and front door. Not to mention the back as well. We spent most of the day swapping shifts of two hours each while the one not on watch caught up on missed sleep from the night before.

Late in the afternoon, Corry left. She was dressed in a long red dress and climbed into the back of a black SUV. We followed her into Antwerp, where the SUV stopped outside a large restaurant. She alighted after the driver opened the door for her. Then she disappeared inside.

I said into my comms, "Slick, you still awake?"

"It's nineteen hundred, Reaper, of course I'm awake."

"The target just went into a restaurant named Heet Specerij. Can you get eyes inside?"

"I'm going to need you to spell it out, Reaper. Your Dutch sucks."

I spelled the title and he came back to me in a few minutes. "No can do, Reaper."

"Roger that."

Taking my Glock out, I put it in the glove compartment. Knocker looked at me and said, "You're not doing what I think you are?"

"I want to know what she's up to."

"I'm coming with you."

"No, stay here. Just keep me tuned in."

I went inside and was thankful the restaurant had a bar. Walking up to it, I found a stool and sat down. A waitress approached me and asked, "What would you like, sir?"

"Scotch," I replied.

"Ice?"

"No, straight up."

"Yes, sir."

While she was getting my drink, I looked around and

saw Corry sitting alone at a table, sipping a glass of wine. "I've got her."

"Good. I bet you also have a glass of booze."

"Got to blend in."

"Asshole."

The waitress brought my drink and took my money. The whiskey was smooth and tasted good. I finished it and then ordered another one. Corry was still seated alone, drinking her wine, and checking the diamond-encrusted watch on her wrist.

"It looks like she's waiting for someone," I said over my comms. "I guess they're late."

"How sad," Knocker said sarcastically.

Corry finished her wine, and I had an idea. I turned around and searched for the waitress. Gaining her attention, she came over to me. "Sir?"

"Can I have a glass of champagne. Make sure it has bubbles."

She returned and I paid for it. Meanwhile, I had Knocker in my ear. "Reaper, you aren't going to approach the target, are you?"

"You know me," I said.

"This is a bad fucking idea, Reaper."

"It's only bad if you get caught."

"Jesus Christ. This is bollocks."

I picked up both drinks and walked between the square tables to the one where Corry was seated. Romantic I am not. Pickup lines usually consist of words along the lines of, do you want to ride in my truck. So, I said, "I noticed you were empty?"

She looked up at me with a quizzical expression. Her eyes took my breath away. They were ice blue. It was then that I noticed that her dark hair was dyed that color. I guess she was blonde beneath it. Her dress was low cut, and I could see the pale flesh of her breasts on either side of the sternum and ribs.

"I beg your pardon?" she asked in accented English.

I held out the glass of champagne. "I hope you like bubbles."

"I'm sorry, but I'm waiting for someone."

"My apologies. I just couldn't abide such a beautiful woman sitting by herself without buying you a drink. I hope you'll accept it and I'll go on my way."

I placed the glass on the table next to the floral center-piece. As I turned and started to walk away, she said, "Excuse me?"

Stopping, I turned back. "Yes?"

"I didn't get your name."

"John."

"Thank you, John. I'm Corry Van Beek."

"Pleased to meet you, Corry. John Roberts."

Back at the bar, I ordered another whiskey. In my ear, Knocker said, "Your pickup lines are shit. I almost vomited in my lap."

"I suppose you can do better?"

"I just couldn't abide such a beautiful woman sitting by herself without buying you a drink. You might as well just shout, I want to fuck you."

"You're exaggerating—wait."

Corry was approaching me, her lithe form weaving between the tables as she walked. She stopped in front of me and said, "It seems I've been stood up. Would you like to join me, John?"

"I'd be lying if I said I was sorry that you were stood up. Their loss is my gain. I would love to join you." I looked down at my casual attire. "That is if you don't mind being seen with a slovenly foreigner."

"I think we can overlook it."

We sat down and talked about various things. We ordered meals and ate, continuing the discussion about nothing. If I didn't know what Corry did, I would have found her quite normal, even alluring. "Why are you in Antwerp, John?" Corry asked as she placed her knife and fork on her plate.

"Business," I replied.

"What kind of business?"

"I investigate tax fraud," I replied.

Her eyes widened for a fraction as her warning senses switched up a gear. "Really? That must be exciting."

"It is boring, actually. All I get to do is look through books at different numbers, trying to piece them together. I should have just remained as an accountant. At least I had the danger of an angry customer every now and then. The only issue I have these days is the savage encounter with the odd paper cut."

Corry smiled and then laughed. "Interesting, but strange."

"What is?"

"That an accountant like you would have tattoos on his arms. I saw part of one when your shirt sleeve moved up."

"A leftover from my first job," I told her. "I was a soldier."

She reached out and touched my hand. "Oh my, you just keep getting even more interesting."

"It wasn't much. I lasted two years before I got out and studied for my accountancy." I stood up. "Please, excuse me. I'll be right back."

"Certainly."

As I walked away from the table, I could feel her eyes burning holes in my back. "Slick, are you there?"

"Hearing every word, Reaper."

"I have a feeling she's about to make a call."

"The cell she has is dialing now."

I went to the bathroom, Slick talking me through it all. "She's called one of her people to do a check on you."

"That could be interesting."

"It would have been if I wasn't one step ahead. As soon as you went down that path, I was making up a false ID as you spoke. You were cutting it damn fine."

"I knew I could count on you."

"She's asking about a background check on you."

"Okay. Is that it?"

"That's it," Slick replied.

"All right, I'll head back."

"Just what is your plan, Reaper?" Knocker asked, cutting in.

"I don't know, I haven't thought that far ahead."

I went back to the table and Corry was waiting for me. She looked up and said, "Shall we have dessert?"

"Why not," I replied, smiling. "What do you recommend?"

"Sit down and we'll see."

We had dessert and talked some more. I looked at my watch and said, "I must go. Thank you for a delightful evening, Corry. Maybe we could have lunch tomorrow? If you're not too busy, that is."

"I'm sorry, John, but I have business to conduct tomorrow, and then I'm flying back to Paris."

"Oh, well, you can't blame a guy for trying."

"However," Corry said slowly. "How about a nightcap before you go back to wherever you are staying?"

"I—"

"Don't worry, I'll have my driver drop you when we're done."

"In that case, I would be honored."

Corry placed her napkin on the table and said, "Shall we go?"

"This is a bad idea, Reaper," Knocker said. "A bad idea."

CHAPTER 16

ONCE IN THE BACK OF CORRY'S SUV, SHE SAT SO OUR LEGS were touching each other. We talked all the way back to her villa, her gaze holding mine. At one point, she reached out and gently touched my thigh before withdrawing her hand.

"Tell me, John, are you going back to America right away after you've completed your business, or are you staying in Europe for a while?"

I shrugged. "I'm not in any rush to get home. There's nothing there waiting for me. Anyway, I should be wrapped up tomorrow."

"How would you like to come to Paris with me?" That almost threw me off my game.

"Are you sure?"

"Totally, I will show you the sights before you have to go home. I'm at a loose end for a few days anyway. After I complete my business tomorrow, we shall leave."

"What is it that you do?"

"I'm in sales."

"Okay."

Her hand found my thigh again and she leaned in close. "Now, enough talk."

Then Corry kissed me, and I knew I was in.

By the time we reached the villa, I had scratched my ear and removed the earwig, putting it into my pocket. The inside of the villa reminded me of a classical home with stone walls and chandeliers. Exposed beams held the ceiling in place, and in the living room, there was a large sofa and an open fireplace with a large rug in front of it.

Once again, we talked and drank and kissed and went to bed.

————

One thing I learned as a Recon Marine was patience. Which came in handy that night as I lay beside Corry waiting for her to be deep in sleep. Over time, her breathing slowed until I was certain I could move without alerting her. She lay naked on the bed, the top sheet covering very little of her lithe body.

I got out of bed and put my clothes on. Her room was large, and the moonlight streamed in through the windows. I'd found out through our conversations that the villa was hers. She used it as she traveled back and forth from Paris.

I went downstairs and walked over to a door, which I knew from her showing me around, that went into her study. I searched through things on top of her desk and through the drawers. That was where I found the ledger.

Closing the curtains, I turned the desk lamp on and began to peruse the book. It was a sales ledger with notations and figures in it. Underneath it, I found a diary. In it for the next day, I found a note for a meeting with MD. Beside it were the words bearer bonds.

I went back to the date and then looked in the ledger. I matched the date and almost fell down. Nine hundred and sixty-five million dollars.

I put them back where I found them, closed the drawer,

and turned the lamp off. I opened the curtain and walked toward the door. Then, instead of going back upstairs, I headed out the front door.

I was met by a guard. He looked at me as he tried to figure out whether to bring up the weapon. I said, "I have to get back to my hotel. Early flight."

He nodded knowingly and watched me leave. As I approached the main gate, I said into my comms, "You awake, Knocker?"

"Wow, it's about fucking time," Knocker growled. "I've been here most of the fucking night."

"I'm on my way out. And I've got some news."

"Do you always sleep with the enemy, Mr. Kane?" German asked.

"Only if I think it will benefit me. I managed to get some information."

"But it didn't do you any good, did it?"

"Not at the time, no."

"That was a stupid move, Kane. Stupid and dumb," Short growled.

"I managed to get information," I told him.

"And most likely tip Corry Van Beek off and make her run."

"That's why we have to act. She has a meeting today with someone with the initials MD," I explained. "She has also marked down in her ledger over nine hundred million in bearer bonds. I think she's buying a shitload of diamonds. That amount can only come from one place."

"You think the diamonds are from the DRC?" Short asked.

"It makes sense," said Holly.

"Why not South Africa or Sierra Leone?"

"Come on, Short," Knocker snapped. "You don't believe that any more than we fucking do."

"What do you propose?"

"Knocker and I go in and pick her up. Bring her out and question her."

"Then what?"

"Give her to Interpol. I'm sure they would like to question her about something," I replied.

"I think the idea is sound, Brian," Holly said.

"All right. Put together a plan and execute it. Find yourself a van, and the four of you go."

"We can run it from here," Holly said.

"No, I want you on-site calling the shots just in case something goes wrong."

Holly nodded. "Okay."

It took us another hour to get ready. Knocker and I grabbed body armor, ammo, and our M6A2s. Climbing into the van, we all left for the villa, pulling up on the far side of the grounds. From the cargo bay where Knocker and I were, I said, "How are we looking, Slick?"

"Hang on a moment, Reaper, I'll have the feed up." His response didn't sound very confident.

I waited patiently. Sitting across from me, Knocker was tapping his fingers on the receiver of his weapon. It was something he did when he was getting impatient. "Come on, Slick, what's the holdup?"

"I can't get a look inside," he replied.

"Can't link, or what?"

"Can't get anything. It's been disabled or jammed or something."

"Fuck," I snarled and pulled the van door open. "Come on, Knocker. We need to get in there."

"What's happening, John?" Holly asked.

"I'm not sure, but I hope it's not what I think it is."

We went over the stone wall and into the grounds. I led

while Knocker drew rear security. Sweeping left and right for targets as I moved, I saw the first body. It was a black lump lying on the grass. "Knocker, I've got a body."

"Copy."

Kneeling beside it, I checked it over. It was one of the guards. He'd been shot several times. "Head on a swivel, Knocker."

"Roger that. Looks like someone beat us to it."

"Yeah. Ghost Lead, it looks like we could have an active shooter on the grounds. Maybe more than one."

"Copy, Ghost One."

We pressed forward toward the villa. There was another dead guard near the pool, and when we went around the front, the guard I'd seen when I'd left was dead on the steps. I looked up and the door was open.

"Open door, Knocker."

"I see it," he replied.

Heading inside, we found the entry empty. The first room on our right was the study, and it was also clear.

From there, we went across the entry to another room and found it empty as well.

Clearing the bottom floor, we found a dead guard in the kitchen. Knocker kicked a spent casing on the floor, and it rattled across the tiles. He bent down and picked something up. "Nine by thirty-nine, Reaper," he said, holding up the round. "Had a jam by the looks of it and cleared it out."

"Russian hit team," I said.

"Has to be. Where do you think she is?"

"Upstairs," I replied.

We took the staircase to the second floor, clearing the rooms as we traversed the hallway. Corry was in her bedroom, still naked from the night before. Obviously, she'd been asleep when the shooters had come in. She looked pale against the blood-soaked sheets. There were three bullet holes in her chest.

"Well, I guess she had two bangs in the last twelve hours," Knocker said grimly.

I glared at him.

"What?"

"Just shut up."

"Too soon?"

I walked over to the window and looked out. "Ghost Lead, we've found the target. She's dead."

"Roger that, John."

"We're going to take a few minutes and see what we can find. Out."

"Copy."

We went back down the stairs and into the study. I headed straight for the desk and opened the drawer. The ledger and diary were still there. I picked them up and said to Knocker, "Let's go."

———

When we got back to the van, Holly asked, "What happened?"

"The Russians beat us to the punch."

"How could they do that?"

"Because they were fucking told," Knocker said. "And guess which prick it was."

"We don't know it was him," Holly replied.

"You're right," I said. "We don't. But it was."

"We need proof, John."

"Don't worry, I'll get it."

We drove back to the apartment, and once we were parked, we went inside. As we climbed the stairs, I noticed something on the concrete. "Stop."

"What's wrong?"

I took out my Glock. "Bloody footprint on the stairs."

Knocker drew his own weapon and went the rest of the

way first. Edging his way to the door of the apartment, he found it open. He went inside and I followed him. We cleared the apartment and went back to the living room part. Short was tied to a chair. His throat had been cut, and he'd been shot in the chest twice.

"You figure he was the target, Reaper?" Knocker asked.

"Yeah, I think so. I'd say he was too much of a liability."

"Oh god," Holly gasped. "Was it them?"

"I think so. Does this place—" Holly was staring wide-eyed at her dead boss. "Holly."

Her head snapped around. "Yes?"

"Does this place have hidden cameras?"

She nodded vaguely. "Y-yes."

"Where?"

"I'll show you."

"Don't show me, show Slick. Then make a call to get a cleanup crew in here."

Holly showed Slick where the cameras were and, once he accessed the feed, showed me what was on them. Three men entered the apartment. It looked like Short was expecting them. "Do we have sound?"

Slick shook his head. "No."

"Why not?"

He shrugged.

As we watched, a fourth man entered. My stare hardened. "Knocker."

He came over and stood beside me. "Fuck, it's him."

It was The Russian.

We continued watching the screen. For a moment, all four men seemed to be talking, but then something changed, and Short was tied to a chair, struggling to free himself. The man we knew as The Russian walked around and stood in front of him. He asked Short some more questions and waited for an answer. When it wasn't forthcoming, he asked him again. I could see his lips moving. Short's head shaking from side to side. Then one of the other Russian men came up behind him and slashed his throat, blood spurting all over the floor and pouring down Short's shirt front.

The man we knew as The Russian drew his suppressed firearm and shot him twice in the chest. Then he put it away, and the small group left the apartment.

"That was fucking brutal," Knocker said.

"It must have been bad to drag The Russian out of his hole."

"Do you think he was here for the diamonds and payment with Corry?"

"Possibly. Slick, I want you to hook into the security cameras at the hotel. If anything weird is going on, I want to know about it."

Slick nodded. "I should know inside a few minutes."

"There is one other thing, Reaper," Knocker said.

"What's that?"

"They're going to need a new diamond buyer. One with access to almost a billion dollars in bearer bonds."

"We're back to where we started. But first things first, Slick, find that bastard."

————

Packing our things, we moved to another residence in Antwerp while the MI6 team cleaned up the Short mess. As far as I knew, he had no family and no one to mourn him. While Slick was hunting for our Russian friend, I had him running a deep dive into Short.

"Reaper, I think the tree has finally given up some fruit," he said to me after an hour of digging.

"What did you find? Our Russian friend?"

"No. But Short had several overseas accounts which totaled three million pounds."

"There's our mole. Can you trace the money back to its origin?"

Slick shook his head. "No. I'm guessing he was paid in cash."

"At least it's been confirmed. Slick, let's assume our Russian is the one in the diary known as MD. Concentrate on that and see what pops."

"Sure. I'll—whoa."

"What is it?"

"Look at this."

I looked and saw our Russian entering the hotel we were expecting him to be at. He was escorted by two men. "Nothing wrong with those cameras."

"No."

"It's like he's laying out the welcome mat," I said.

"It would seem that way."

"All right, let's bite."

—————

I found Holly and told her my plans and about the other developments. She said, "I can't believe that Brian was bad."

"I've learned, as you would have, that nothing should surprise, but it always does. You and Slick should go to the embassy. It will be a lot safer there."

"I think you're right. Just be careful. It could be a trap."

"I have no doubt that it is. The trick is to avoid it."

"One more thing. You said that they would need another dealer. What about the Diamond Exchange? We have feed of Noskov being there."

"I doubt they would handle almost a billion dollars in diamonds in one hit. I think we're looking for a lone wolf dealer like Corry Van Beek."

"I'll see what I can find out."

———

We picked out two vehicles before we even moved from the SUV we were in. A dark Mercedes sedan and a black Range Rover. "Slick, do you have them?"

"Yes, sir."

"I can't tell how many in each, but I think they're it."

"I've got a lone wolf directly across the street," Knocker said.

"Got him," I replied.

"Before you go in, I've picked up something weird in the feed," Slick said cautiously.

"Go ahead."

"The cameras were tampered with before your Russian friend went inside. Then they came good."

"Did you figure out where The Russian went?"

"That's another strange thing. He went to room four-oh-eight. The cameras showed him going in."

"What about coming out?" I asked.

"Yes. But get this, he looked up at the camera as he did. It was as though he wanted us to know he was there."

I thought for a moment and Knocker said, "I don't like it. He came and went and didn't care who saw."

"That's because the only ones looking for him are us. He wants us to know he was in there and he wants us to go and see what he was up to."

Knocker checked his Glock and put spare magazines into his pockets. "Let's go find out what the bastard wanted to show us."

Heading inside the hotel, we turned left to access the elevators. I pressed the call button, and when it arrived, we climbed into the first one. We were the only ones in it. The ascent was smooth, the warning bell chime indicating we'd reached the correct level. I followed Knocker out.

The room we wanted was on the right, about halfway

along the carpeted corridor. The big numbers greeted us when we stopped, along with the do not disturb sign. Knocker tried the door, and it snicked open. He immediately drew the Glock from the back of his pants, and I followed suit.

We could smell the blood before we saw it. I heard Knocker mutter something as he moved further into the room.

There were two bodies. Like Short, they had been shot and their throats cut. Knocker glanced back at me and said, "It's them."

"Yeah. Pierre and Francois."

"What's happening, John?" Holly asked.

"Our two friends from Interpol have been murdered, Holly. You'd better get someone here."

"Oh, no. Why would they do this?"

"They're sending us a message." I stared at the bodies again. "Fuck."

"Reaper, you've got four assholes coming your way," Slick said. "My guess is that they're armed."

"Copy. Knocker, we've got visitors incoming."

He looked over at me and said, "Let them fucking come. They've got me really pissed now."

So, we waited. Took up positions inside the room with the door open and waited. The first came with a warning from Slick. The second was the shadow that fell across the floor from the doorway. I was lying beside the bed, Knocker, the sofa. The four of them entered and looked around.

"Where are they?" one asked in Russian.

"Right fucking here, comrade," Knocker snarled and opened fire.

His first shots took the speaker down. The man fell forward and crashed to the floor, his eyes wide with shock.

My first shots came from the side, and brains from the second assassin sprayed the wall.

Knocker helped the third killer to hell the express way. Three bullets to the head. Each shot crashed out deafeningly. The fourth killer cried out something in Russian that I didn't understand because it synchronized with my final four shots. Two to the chest, one to the throat, and the last smashed into his open mouth, out of the back of his head, and into the wall.

Our weapons covered the doorway just in case. "Slick, confirm four?"

"Roger, Reaper. Confirm four."

"In that case, we're clear here."

I looked at the carnage all around us. It was a ghastly sight. Knocker said, "We need to put a stop to this, Reaper. And quick."

CHAPTER 17

"You are not going to believe this," Slick said to me as I lay on my bed, half asleep. It had been a long twenty-four hours of interrogation by the Antwerp police until we were released the following day.

"What aren't I going to believe, Slick?" I asked tiredly.

"Our Russian friend has a name." I sat up. I could see the excitement in his eyes. "It took some doing, but I got a match. His name is Misha Durov."

"Are you sure?"

"Hell, yes."

I thought for a moment. We knew of three generals, and now we had names for them. Shatov, Noskov, and now Misha Durov. "What did you find out, Slick?"

"Durov, back in the day, commanded the 68th Army Corps. From there, he went to the Kremlin. He disappeared after that."

"Did he die?" I asked.

"I could find no record of anything."

Feeling my anger begin boiling inside of me, I said, "Fuck it. Slick, you do whatever it is you have to do, but you find Durov. Find him."

"Yes."

Holly was going through Corry's diary and ledger, and I looked over at her and asked, "You find anything?"

"I found out that the bitch was disgustingly rich," she replied. "It also looks as though she met with Noskov on the day the cameras glitched, and there are entries about the diamond exchange as well."

"What about it?"

"She freelances for them. The day Noskov went in, she was on-site."

"How many stones?"

"Five hundred thousand dollars."

"That can't be right," I said. "Five hundred thousand to almost a billion dollars is a big jump."

"Not if it was a taste," Holly said. "The first case was cash. Organize to meet her at his hotel for a bigger cache. According to the diary and ledger she did ten million in bearer bonds. This one was meant to be the big one. Almost a billion dollars. But with her on-selling them, she could take the amount up to one point five."

"So Durov is somewhere in Antwerp with all these diamonds, looking for another buyer."

"It seems that way. He won't want to take them back with him."

"Then he'll need someone to set it up. The question is, who?"

Holly said, "I can make a few calls and see what I learn."

I nodded. "Okay."

Twenty minutes later, Holly came to me and said, "Feel like a ride?"

"Where are we going?"

"To see a local mobster," she explained. "He might be able to point us in the right direction."

"Let's go then."

———

We took the SUV and headed into the city. The sun was going down in the west and the orange streetlamps were coming on. "Where are we going?"

"A gentlemen's club."

"That could be interesting," I allowed. "A woman in a gentlemen's club."

"Do you think I should walk in dressed just in my underwear?" Holly asked.

"Sure, I'll wait outside and catch you as they throw you out."

When we arrived, Holly parked the SUV in the gravel lot. The club looked more like a stone-built mansion estate out of some 1920s television show. We climbed out and headed inside. The desk in the foyer was manned by a guy in his fifties. He took one look at Holly and said, "No."

"We're here to see Michel Sonck."

She started toward the lounge.

"Wait!"

We turned back toward him. "I will get him for you."

He disappeared through the door into the lounge. I looked at Holly and nodded. "You almost gave him a heart attack."

"I possibly would have had one if I'd gone in there."

A couple of minutes later, the old man returned with a much larger man who wore a mustache like Dick Dastardly. Looking us both over, he waved a thick cigar in the air and asked, "What do you want?"

"Information," Holly said.

Sonck snorted derisively. "Fuck off. Who do you think you are?"

"I'm the person who can turn your life upside down and make everything disappear," Holly said.

He clicked his fingers. "And I can have you killed just like that."

"Only if you beat me to it."

"You are very confident for a whore."

Holly smiled coldly. "And you're a fucking asshole. Now that we're done with the insults, is there somewhere we can talk?"

He looked at me and gave a wry grin. "I like her." Then to Holly, "I like you."

"Come on, Michel. I'm getting tired."

"Follow me."

He took us upstairs into a private lounge. "What information do you want?"

"Top-end diamond buyers," Holly said.

"You are in Antwerp. Take your pick," he said jovially.

"Come on, Michel. Someone who uses bearer bonds."

"Again, Antwerp." He shrugged.

"The sellers will have almost a billion dollars in stones," I said to him.

That got his attention. "Corry Van Beek."

"She's dead, but you know that," Holly shot back at him.

He nodded. "It depends."

"Depends on what?"

"Who is selling."

"Russians," I replied.

"You joke. Russians never have that much in diamonds."

My gaze was unwavering. He looked at Holly. "Is he serious?"

"The same ones were responsible for the murder of Corry Van Beek and two Interpol officers."

He shook his head. "Wait, who are you?"

"British Intelligence."

"Why is British Intelligence involved with diamonds?" Sonck asked.

"Don't worry about that. Just give us a name."

He stared at Holly for a long moment before nodding. "Enzo Gerets. If anyone can handle that kind of money, it's him."

Holly nodded. "Thank you."

"Don't thank me. Corry Van Beek was an angel compared to him. If you get hold of him, kill him when you are finished. If you don't, he will come after you. And believe me, he will kill you."

"Do you know where we can find him?" I asked.

"You don't," Sonck said. "You have to have something he wants, and then you have to set up a meeting through his middleman. Or, in this case, his middle woman."

"What's her name?"

"Feli Tysiak."

"Where do we find her?"

"Antwerp Museum of Antiquities."

We got to our feet. "Thanks for your help, Michel."

"Take my advice, kill Enzo when you are done."

Leaving the club, we went back to our SUV. We climbed in just as a light rain was starting to fall from a leaden sky. Holly said, "We're going to need diamonds."

I frowned. "Why?"

"Because she isn't going to put us in touch with Gerets without showing her a sample of what we have."

She was right. "Where do we get diamonds from?"

"The only place I can think of," Holly said.

"Where's that?"

"We steal them."

"Now just hold on a minute," Holland blurted out. "You were going to steal diamonds to help you get a meet with a dangerous criminal?"

I shook my head. "No."

"Good."

"We did."

His eyes widened. "That is preposterous."

"We did what we had to do."

"You're nothing but common criminals."

"Oh, do be quiet, Jack," Christine Ryan snapped. *"They were doing what they had to do to get the job done. Continue. Don't skip over the diamond robbery. It's not in the file and I want to hear about it."*

His name was Alexander Boccard. He was a diamond merchant who made one mistake that left him vulnerable. He used to take his work home with him. No matter what day it was, whenever he left work, he carried a sum of diamonds in his briefcase. Most of the time it averaged around $100,000's worth.

Holly said, "Don't ask me why he does it, because I have no idea. I think he's just egotistical. He's got the goods and carrying them around like that probably gives him a hard-on."

"I guess he's about to feel the droop," Knocker said.

We sat in the SUV, waiting for the dealer to emerge from his place of business. When he did, it was in a dark blue Mercedes sedan. Leaving the underground parking garage, once he hit the street, he turned right. Holly pulled away from the sidewalk and fell in behind him.

We followed his vehicle for a couple of blocks and once we were where we wanted to be, executed the robbery.

He stopped at an intersection and Holly rolled up on him and gave him a nudge with the front bumper. As soon as it happened, Knocker and I pulled our ski masks down and leaped from the vehicle.

We had our weapons out and walked steadily up each side of the Mercedes. But he saw us coming and locked his doors. Trying the door handles, we found they wouldn't let us in. His foot dropped onto the gas pedal and the Mercedes lurched forward.

"Slick, kill the fucking car."

"On it."

The Mercedes motor stopped halfway through the intersection, and it rolled to a standstill. Knocker and I ran forward. I heard him growl, "Motherfucker."

We tried the doors, but they were still locked. Through the tinted window, I could see Alexander fumbling with his cell. Grinding my teeth in frustration, I smashed the window on the passenger side and reached in, grabbing the briefcase.

I managed to extract it before he realized it was the diamonds we wanted and not him. Holly pulled up beside us, waited for us to leap in, then she sped off, leaving an angry and confused diamond merchant behind us.

"Shit a fucking brick, Reaper, that is why we don't do stuff like that in broad daylight," Knocker snapped.

"Are you both okay?" Holly asked.

"Yes," I replied. "We're fine."

"Tomorrow, we move to the next part of the plan."

"Durov could be back in fucking Russia by now with some prostitute sitting on his face," Knocker snapped. "Or drinking vodka martinis in some bloody Siberian shack."

"He's still here," I said. "I can feel the bastard."

———

I slept badly that night, my mind not switching off as I ran through everything we had done and had yet to do. What we knew at that time was that the deal in Syria was to get at a new oil field. The DRC was all about diamonds and money. Something they obviously needed. There were five generals, of which we knew Shatov, Noskov, and now Misha Durov. The worrying factor was the network they had set up. They had the ability to reach out and touch anyone they chose to. Even the ability to place their own pawn in the top job in Russia.

The more I thought about it, the more I was convinced

they were building up to something big and that Knocker was right. If they were preparing for war, what was their ultimate goal? And surely, they knew that NATO wouldn't have any of it. There were still a lot of blank spaces that needed to be filled in.

That was why we needed to find Durov.

The following morning, I was drinking coffee with Knocker when Holly appeared with a concerned expression on her face. "That's a look that bespeaks trouble," I said.

"That's because we've been ordered back to London."

"By who?" I asked.

"Christine Ryan," she replied.

"The stupid cow that shifted Short to the right instead of shuffling his ass off to prison?" Knocker snarled.

Christine Ryan stared at Knocker. Actually, glared was a more accurate description. Fire blazed in her eyes, but my friend just shrugged his shoulders. "I stand by my words. You should have put the prick in prison instead of reassigning him."

She surprised us by saying, "I agree. But that is all water under the bridge."

"Very tumultuous water by my reckoning," Knocker mumbled into his beard.

Holly said, "She is about to move up to the intelligence committee, so I hear."

"Well, whoever thought that was a good idea isn't very intelligent, shit."

"Can we skip that part, Mr. Kane? I'm sure we don't need to know every intricate detail that's not relevant."

"Ignore it," I said. "We're too close to this thing to be taken out of the game now."

"I can't just ignore the order."

"Then don't. You go back and convince her that we need to be here. Meanwhile, Knocker, Slick, and I will keep doing what we're doing."

"I'm not sure that is a good idea, John."

"We'll be fine," Knocker said. "I promise we won't blow anything up until you get back."

Holly rolled her eyes. "That instills me with a great deal of confidence."

"We have to keep the pressure on these people, Holly," I said to her. "If we don't, then they can do whatever they want at will. Durov is in Antwerp. We haven't been this close for a while. If we can get him, then who knows, we just might be able to wrap this thing up."

"Who are you going to use as the diamond dealer to get to Feli Tysiak?"

"Slick."

———

"Come on, Reaper, can't you use Raymond?" Slick whined.

"Look at him. Does he look like a diamond dealer?"

"He looks—"

"Like a drunk who just got off a train," I finished for him.

"Thanks a lot," came Knocker's vexed reply.

"You're the only one who can do it," Holly said. "I have to go back to London."

He looked at us with worried eyes. "You know I'm at home behind a computer."

"You'll be fine. I'll be right there with you."

"Fine."

———

We got Holly on her flight back to London and then went to the museum to see Feli. Knocker found a park, and we put earwigs in to remain in contact. I looked at my friend and said, "Try to stay out of trouble."

"You know me."

"Yeah, I do, that's why I said it."

Slick and I went inside. The main reception area was huge. Complete with sculptures, paintings, and even a vase that could have been Ming Dynasty or something fake just for display. We were both well-dressed in suits. Slick carried the briefcase with the diamonds inside.

"Over there, Slick," I said. "The guy in the green suit. He looks like he belongs here."

"I guess we'll find out."

We approached the man in question, who saw us coming while we were still a distance away. He smiled, revealing a gap-toothed grin. "Can I help you?" he asked in Dutch.

"Ah, do you speak English?" Slick asked him.

"Yes, yes. Can I help you?"

"We're here to see Feli Tysiak," Slick said, sounding less than confident.

"Can I ask what it is about? Miss Tysiak is a very busy lady."

"Business."

"Yes?" He waited, expecting us to be more forthcoming with our answer.

"Our own," Slick said.

He nodded. "Yes, I'm sorry. I will see if she is available."

Green suit disappeared and left us standing there waiting. I whispered to Slick, "You did well."

"My hands are sweaty, and my throat is dry. I haven't felt like this since that gunfight you got me into in Yemen."

"That wasn't me, that was Knocker."

"You were there," Slick said.

"Wasn't my fault," Knocker said over the comms. "Slick stared too long at that terrorist's wife. Pissed him off. If it hadn't been for me, he would have been killed."

"You shot him in the head," Slick pointed out.

"Better him than you."

"Head's up," I said as a woman in an emerald pantsuit

appeared. She had flowing red hair and pale skin. "Damn, Slick, looks like you two have something in common."

"Yeah, good one."

"Hello, gentlemen. I'm Feli Tysiak. I was told you wanted to see me." Her smile showed a mouthful of even white teeth.

"Yes, ma'am," Slick replied.

If I could have, I would have slapped him up the back of the head. However, Knocker did that verbally. "Hey, shit-head, tell her your bloody name, you goose."

"Yes, I'm Brian Rogers. I was hoping we could discuss a matter of great urgency?"

"What would that be?"

"A matter of some valuable merchandise I have in my briefcase."

She gave him a wan smile and said, "I'm sorry, I cannot help you."

As she turned away Slick said desperately, "Half a million dollars' worth."

Feli stopped and stared at him. Her mind was ticking over as she fought internally with the decision to make. "All right, follow me."

She took us through the museum to a door with a sign that I can only assume said staff only, for on the other side was a hallway with doors on either side leading into offices.

Feli found the one she wanted and opened the door, stepping to one side to allow us to enter. She turned and closed the door behind us. Inside the office was a large wooden, hand-tooled desk. My guess was that it had been created from a tree felled in an ancient forest. She sat down in a chair and indicated to the only other one there for Slick to use. I stood post to the left of the door.

"Now, Mr. Rogers, why do you think I can help you?"

"I was told you could."

"In what way?" Feli asked, raising a questioning eyebrow.

"I was told you could put me in touch with a buyer for my diamonds?"

"The buyers I deal with don't get out of bed for a mere half a million in diamonds."

Knocker said in his ear, "Slick, tell her it's just a sample. Tell her you have five million."

"I have more," he said to her. "I was told that you wouldn't consider anything without seeing some of the stones. Half a million is what I have on me."

"How much do you have in total?" Feli asked.

"Five million."

"Still a little light, Mr. Rogers," she replied.

Slick licked his lips nervously. Knocker said, "Tell her there will be more next time. Triple."

"There will be more next time. Triple of what I will have now."

"Really?" she asked skeptically. "Where from?"

"Tell her Sierra Leone," Knocker said.

"Ah…"

Feli raised her eyebrows. "Hmm?"

"Tell her, damn it. Christ, you'll fuck it up."

"Sierra Leone."

"Are you telling me they are conflict diamonds, Mr. Rogers?"

"No, no. They are all above board."

I stared at Feli, trying to gauge her. She must have sensed my stare because her eyes flicked over to me. She did the down-up thing, taking me all in, and then said, "Maybe I can help you, Mr. Rogers."

"Great. I do hope so," Slick replied.

"You'd better show me your diamonds."

Slick placed the briefcase on Feli's desk and opened it. He then took out the sack of diamonds and a black velvet cloth, laying the cloth down before emptying the stones onto it. Feli picked one up and examined it using a loupe. She put the diamond down and picked up another. For the next few minutes, Feli repeated the process until she was satisfied. "I think I have seen enough." Her eyes fell upon me. "Almost enough."

"Then you will set up a meeting with a buyer?"

"Yes. I have someone in mind."

"Thank you."

Again, she devoured me with her eyes while Slick put the diamonds away. "No, thank you. Give me your number and I'll call you within the hour."

Slick gave her the number for a burner phone we had, and our business with Feli Tysiak concluded. Now all we had to do was wait for her call.

CHAPTER 18

True to her word, Feli Tysiak called within the hour, having set up a buyer for us. "You will meet him at the old football stadium in east Antwerp in two hours. Do not be late or he will leave."

"Who is the buyer?" Slick asked. "I need a name to make sure I'm not getting ripped off."

"Enzo Gerets," Feli said after a moment of hesitation. "A word of warning. Do not mess with him. He is a very dangerous man."

"Thank you for your help," Slick said and disconnected the call.

With a nod of satisfaction, I said, "Good. We're almost there. Knocker, get your kit and get out there. I want you in position before Gerets arrives. No doubt he'll have the same idea."

"On my way, Reaper. What do you want me to do if he has men show?"

"Mark them and see what they do. Don't take them out unless you have to. Make sure you have a laser. I want Gerets on edge while we talk."

"I think I can manage that."

Knocker left and I turned to Slick. "Are you going to be okay?"

"I guess."

"I'll be there with you. But you'll need a gun."

"Make it a big one."

Two hours later, we entered the football stadium. Knocker saw us arrive and said into our comms, "I'm up near the scoreboard, Reaper."

"Copy. Did Gerets send anyone ahead?"

"I've got two on overwatch with DMRs. I can get a clear shot at them if need be. I've got you covered."

"Roger that." I turned to Knocker. "Now we wait."

It didn't take long for them to appear. They were on the other side of the old pitch up in the stand, starting to come down. I knew their intent and said to Slick, "Onto the pitch."

We walked down the stairs and through the small gate which led onto the ankle length grass that had once seen international football matches. I had Slick on my left so he would be clear of my gun arm if I had to pull the Glock. I said in a low voice, "Knocker, we good?"

"Roger that."

We walked toward the three men opposite, reaching the middle at the same time. Gerets stared at us for a long moment. "I hope you make this worth my while, or someone will pay."

"Look down at your chest, Enzo," I said in a low voice.

"What?" He stared at the red pinpoint dot and looked back up. "What the hell is going on?"

I said, "I'm going to have my man kill you if you don't answer a couple of questions for me."

He surprised me with a cold smile. "You have no idea who you are dealing with, do you?"

"A dead man if you don't participate." He glowered at us. "And don't worry about your men in the stands, we know they are there."

That just seemed to inflame him more. "It was you, wasn't it?"

"Me, what?"

"Murdered Corry and her people."

I shook my head. "No, that was someone else."

Gerets's eyes narrowed. "Who?"

"If I'm right, the same people who are going to be selling you almost a billion dollars in diamonds."

His eyes flickered. "I do not know what you are talking about."

"They're Russian. They're looking to offload a shitload of diamonds from the DRC. Except they get their money in bearer bonds, they'll kill you because they don't like loose ends."

"How do you know this?"

"It just came to me. As soon as they find out we were here, they'll make a concerted effort to kill you."

Gerets remained silent.

"They contacted you, didn't they?"

He nodded.

"Did he tell you his name was Durov?"

"Yes."

"Then you're screwed. The only way you get out of this is for us to help each other."

"Why should I trust you?"

"Because you have to."

"What is it you propose?"

"Keep the meeting and we'll be there to take out Durov and his people," I explained.

"Fine."

"When is the meeting?"

"Tomorrow night at the new apartment complex building site," Gerets told me.

I said, "Fine. We'll be there, you just won't see us."

"How do I know I can trust you?"

I tapped Slick on the shoulder. "Give him the case."

"What's that?" Gerets asked.

"There's half a million worth of diamonds inside. You can have them. We just want Durov."

He took the case and left without another word. As we were leaving, Knocker joined us. He said, "Do you think you can trust him?"

"Not a hope in hell."

———

"Meanwhile, as we waited, Holly landed in London and was taken by car to see the woman who had called her back. Anything you want to add before I go on?" I asked Christine Ryan.

"You all were meant to be with her."

"We couldn't leave in the middle of what we were doing," I said.

"You were creating a mess."

"We were getting close," Holly said.

"Do you have anything to add?" Christine Ryan asked Knocker.

"No, ma'am. You know how I feel."

"Yes, you made that all too obvious."

Holly said, *"When I was brought into HQ, I explained what was happening at the time."*

"All you had were theories. You had nothing concrete."

"A village—an entire village—was murdered, and the oil that was discovered shipped back to Russia. Then came the issue in the DRC. Billions of dollars in diamonds, all of them ready to be sold to buyers in Antwerp."

"*But it was still theory.*"

"*What about Georgy? He confirmed to us about the generals. We had three names at the time. All of them long-dead or disappeared. These men weren't just operating in the shadows, they were ghosts. It was only by luck that we found them in the first place. Their setup was better than our own intelligence services.*"

"*Are you finished?*" German asked dismissively.

I stared hard at Christine Ryan and said, "*While we were otherwise engaged, Holly was being needlessly interrogated back here. We were hamstrung and compromised because of it. What happened next was just as much your fault as it was ours.*"

"*You blew up a train.*"

"*Yes, we fucking did.*"

We were in position just after dark. The building site was deserted, and we took up positions where we could cover the meeting. Knocker and I were armed with M6s and had body armor, NVGs, and laser sights. Slick was in the SUV we had hidden nearby.

All the time we were in position we kept alert just in case the Russians slipped in a specialist team. On top of that, Slick had hooked into a satellite which allowed us to cover more area.

"I've got a vehicle approaching, Reaper," he said after we'd been there for a couple of hours.

"Roger that. Keep an eye open for anything that's not right."

The SUV appeared and stopped in the open area where a stack of steel and lumber was situated. Further off to the side was the site office. All four doors opened, and four people got out. It was Gerets and his men.

They stood there in the headlights and waited. Gerets seemed to be looking around, most likely trying to see if we were there. Thirty minutes later, Slick said, "Reaper, I've got three more vehicles coming in fast."

"Okay. Let's keep our heads on a swivel. Knocker, time to go to work, buddy."

"Let's just hope Durov is there."

"We have to take him alive," I said. "Remember that."

The three vehicles came in at speed and skidded to a halt. There was no movement at first, just the dust in the headlights kicked up by the SUVs. Then, after a minute or so, the doors opened, and twelve shooters emerged. Eleven of them were armed and wearing combat gear. Three carried briefcases. One man stood out from the others. He was dressed in a long black coat and a hat. It was Durov.

"These bastards mean business, Reaper," Knocker said to me over his comms.

"Yeah. I wouldn't expect anything else."

"Reaper, I've got movement in the building across from you," Slick said. "Looks like two targets. On the—"

A train went past, slowing down for the nearby station.

"Say again, Slick," I whispered.

"Second floor across from you."

I moved my weapon so I could see the targets he was talking about. At first, I missed them, then I caught the movement beneath a plastic curtain. Two snipers. "Knocker, I've got two shooters on the second floor across from me. Can you see them?"

"I've got them, Reaper. What do you want to do?"

"Just hold for the moment. We'll see how this unfolds."

We watched the meet for a while. Gerets and Durov exchanged words and…

"And what?" Holland asked.

"It's in the report."

"I want to hear it from you, Cowboy."

I stared at him, a sudden violent urge to punch him in the mouth coursing through my veins. "We fucked up. We missed a shooter."

We heard the suppressed shot before we knew what was

happening. Gerets dropped like a stone to the hard-packed ground beneath his feet. The other two shooters opened fire from across the way, and so did Durov's men on the ground.

"Shit," I snarled and fired at one of the two snipers we'd originally seen. I shot one through the head while Knocker got the other. We changed our aim and opened up on Durov's bodyguards.

Before they realized what was happening, we had two more down. Both had been carrying briefcases. I fired at the third mule and put him down too.

"Slick, where's that fucking third sniper?"

"I don't know. I'm trying to find him."

I could hear Knocker's suppressed weapon firing as he picked targets. But the shooters were professionals and they had gathered themselves, taken cover behind their SUVs, and were returning fire.

I looked for Durov but couldn't see him. "Knocker, disable their vehicles. We can't let them leave."

Suddenly a round snapped close to my head. The third sniper had found my position. I rolled to the left and took cover behind a crate. "Slick, that bastard has me pinpointed. Where is he?"

"I'm still looking, Reaper."

WHAP!

"Damn it, Slick."

"I've got him. He's in the third-floor apartment block under construction to your right."

I leaned around and was shot at again. But this time, I picked him out. My weapon came into line, and I fired. That ended his sniping days.

Meanwhile, when I looked at the situation below, bodies lay near the vehicles, but there were still active shooters.

I fired at one of them and said, "Knocker, can you see Durov?"

"No."

A shooter jumped into the lead vehicle and tried to start it, but it wouldn't move. I sighted my M6 on the driver's side windshield and fired a tight group of four rounds. Each found a home in the Russian operator.

"Cover me, Knocker, I'm going down."

Coming to my feet, I ran to the internal stairwell. Moments later, I was on the ground and taking cover behind a concrete pylon. I leaned around it to get an overall look at the situation I was facing. A handful of shooters were still alive, and close to one of them was Durov.

Bringing my M6A2 around, I fired at another of Durov's men. He slumped forward, blood spurting from the throat wound. I heard something bounce nearby and instinct told me to throw myself flat on the ground.

The explosion from the grenade was loud. I felt the concussive blast wave sweep over me along with the heat. I growled a deep-throated curse and fired a long burst in the direction of the Russians.

"Are you all right, Reaper?" Knocker asked.

"I'm still in the fight."

Dragging myself back behind the concrete pylon, I made it just in time as bullets began smashing chunks out of it. I pressed my back against its hardness, thankful that it was something solid between me and them. Then Knocker said, "Reaper, they're squirting."

I looked around and saw Durov disappearing, followed by one of his guards. A curse escaped my lips as a burst of gunfire hammered past me. Grinding my teeth, I emerged from cover and fired at a crouching figure. He cried out and fell back. Apart from the two who had run and one of Gerets's crew, he was the last one alive.

"Slick, secure the diamonds. Knocker, on me."

I didn't want to be running through Antwerp streets in full tactical gear, carrying an assault weapon, so I dumped them and kept the Glock. "Knocker, dump your gear, keep your secondary."

"Roger that, Reaper."

"Slick, make sure you get our gear and weapons."

"Copy."

I ran off the construction site with Knocker close behind me. Almost instantly, we were on the street, and I could see Durov and his guard running in the distance. For an old man, he was making good pace, but the only way he would successfully escape was to disappear. At his age and at that pace, running too far had to be an issue.

"He's headed for the train station," Knocker called out.

Trying to increase our pace, we were still on the street, and a vehicle beeped its horn at us as it went past. The bodyguard turned and fired in our direction, bullets cracking as they passed close. I jinked left and back right. The guard turned and followed his boss.

"If the prick gets on a train, it'll be hell digging him out," Knocker said.

We ran through a parking lot toward the train station's main entrance. As we entered, we put our Glocks away so we wouldn't panic any of the commuters who were milling around. We needn't have bothered. Durov and his man were already doing that.

A whining sound signaled the arrival of the next train. It slowed to a stop, and I saw Durov and his man get on two carriages along. I grabbed Knocker, and we jumped through the closest open carriage door before it closed.

Looking through the passengers toward the end of the carriage, I began pushing my way through in that direction. "Excuse me...excuse me...coming through."

"Hey, what are you doing?"

I gave the speaker a hard stare, and he shrank back from the big guy with the tattoos and beard. "Good idea, mate," I heard Knocker say behind me. "He's having a bad day."

We moved forward through the carriage and into the next one. We were greeted by a wave of frightened people coming the other way.

Struggling against the tide, we reached the next carriage and found it empty. Ahead, I could see into the next, and it too was empty.

I took out my Glock, and Knocker did the same. He said in a low voice, "This could turn into a hostage situation, Reaper?"

"Yeah, it could."

He looked at the ticker above the door. "We've got about five minutes to the next station. It looks like it's an express. The upside is that they are contained, and we don't have to look through passengers getting out of each carriage."

"Then we'd better fucking find them."

Pushing forward to the next carriage, I could see them through the doors. Durov and his man were not alone. They had two hostages, both women. We were too late.

Both women were crying. They were at the far end of the carriage, and we were just inside the bottom doors. "You just don't seem to know when to give up," Durov said.

"Let the ladies go. They have nothing to do with this," I said, taking a step forward.

"Just stay there, or the ladies will die."

"They didn't do anything," I told him.

"But you did. You keep fucking everything up. Now you have our diamonds."

"What's so important about them?"

"They're ours," Durov replied.

"What are you all up to, Durov?"

I'd used his name, and it drew a reaction. He hissed through his teeth. "I suppose you think you are smart? So, you know who I am."

"The thing is, we're putting it all together. Slowly."

"You have nothing," he snarled. Suddenly his man

moved, and something started bouncing along the carriage floor toward us.

"Grenade!" Knocker cried out.

We threw ourselves backward, and the doors closed just as the grenade detonated.

CHAPTER 19

THE DOORS BUCKLED UNDER THE BLAST AND THE WINDOWS blew out, showering us with glass. The carriage we were in rose up and bucked beneath us. Knocker and I were thrown around inside and I hit my ribs against a seat. Feeling them give, I cried out. I was reasonably sure that they didn't break but would be badly bruised.

Knocker hit his head on something, instantly bringing forth a flow of blood. The internal lights flickered and went out, only to flicker on again as the emergency lighting kicked in. The carriage lurched to the side as it derailed. I ground my teeth against more pain as it hit the side of the tunnel, throwing us around some more like peas in a pan.

The inertia of the carriages at the back thrust them forward, and I happened to glance up just in time to see a concrete pylon coming toward us.

"Shit. Move! Move! Move!"

I scrambled back along the aisle, Knocker with me as the pylon tore through the front of the detached carriage. Metal shredded and crunched as it came closer, and for a moment, I thought we were about to die, buried in a crush of metal and concrete.

Then the train stopped, and an eerie silence seemed to settle over us as it does after a moment of chaos. "Knocker, are you all right?"

"That was fucking intense," he replied, shaking his head.

I rolled over and looked at him. "You're bleeding," I said.

"I'm not the only one."

I dragged him to his feet. The carriage was on a lean but not too severe. I looked at the front of the carriage and saw nothing but a crumpled mess. The one in front of it was on fire. "Can't go that way."

We managed to go back and out a side door. Commuters who were able were out on the tracks. The injured were left inside. I looked toward the front of the train, but it was nowhere in sight, having split in two. Knocker said, "We have to get out of here."

"I agree. Slick, can you hear me?"

Static.

"Slick, are you on channel?"

Still nothing. "Knocker, you try."

He had as much success as I did. "We need to get above ground."

We were forced back along the line to an escape door or fire exit. Opening it, we ran up the stairs to another door which opened out onto a street. "Slick, are you there?"

"Copy, Reaper. Where are you?"

I glanced at Knocker. "Where are we?"

"Fucked if I know."

We looked around and saw a street sign with a name that was relayed back to Slick. "Be right there."

He took ten minutes to pick us up. Once we were in the SUV, I asked, "Did you get everything?"

"Sure, but you guys look like shit. What happened?"

"Durov blew up the bloody train," Knocker growled. "But don't worry, we'll get the blame for it."

"We need to find him, Slick."

"Don't worry, we will."

"*Three dead and twenty-four injured,*" German said.

"Sir?"

"*The casualties from the train you blew up.*"

"Technically not true, sir. Durov's man blew it up."

"*You were there.*"

"Yes, and we were still in the fight."

"I've got him," Slick said as he trawled through footage from the night before. "It's Durov sure enough."

"Where is he?"

"There is an old theater in the center of Antwerp. It's abandoned and earmarked for demolition. Security cameras across the street caught them going in. I haven't seen them come out."

"Why do you suppose he went there instead of the embassy?" Knocker asked aloud.

"I have no idea." I looked at the feed Slick had up. It was Durov sure enough.

"Listen to this, Reaper. I managed to pick it up."

"*...killed most of...men. They have...diamonds. ...extract now.*"

"*Christ, Misha...stay...are. I will send...you.*"

"*Hurry, Mikhail. Before...find me.*"

"That's it," Slick said to us.

"We need to get to him before they do." I started getting into my kit. "Slick, you drive. If we get him, we'll need to get out before they turn up."

————

We loaded up and headed into the center of Antwerp. Slick parked on the street, and we paused before getting out. Knocker said what I was thinking. "Too many people, Reaper. If we get out like we're going to war, we'll have police crawling all over us."

"Find us a back way in, Slick."

He started the motor again and pulled away from the sidewalk. Driving around the block, he found an empty lot and pulled into it. The weeds were knee high, and there were mounds of bricks and stone. Off to one side was a large sign about some construction set to start six months down the road.

We got out and checked our comms. "Slick, if this goes south, get the hell out and go to the embassy."

"You won't see me for dust."

Knocker scratched his beard. "I have one of those feelings, Reaper."

"Don't start that shit."

"Fine," he said as he started trudging toward the theater. "Watch my six."

The back door was hanging off its hinges, graffiti painted all over it by a budding artist with too much time on their hands. Inside smelled musty, damp. I think something had died in there because we could smell the sickly sweet scent of decay. Or maybe it was just the rotting wood, exposed to the elements by the hole in the roof. We crept through the rubble in the back rooms where actors changed. From there, we were out onto the stage and there was still no sign of Durov.

Suddenly a shot came and a bullet cut the air between us. We ran for cover in different directions, more bullets punching holes in the loose floorboards of the stage.

"Bollocks," Knocker snarled. "The son of a bitch is up high, Reaper."

I looked for the shooter amongst the balconies of the private boxes but saw nothing. "Knocker, can you see him?"

"Wait, one, I'm still looking for him."

I leaned out over the orchestra pit to try and find the shooter, using the sights on my M6A2. A burst of bullets forced me back.

"Got him, Reaper. Second floor, fourth box on the left. I'm going up. Keep him busy."

Across the stage, I saw Knocker disappear. Raising my weapon in the direction of the area Knocker had said the shooter was, I was forced back once again by bullets, but not for long. I sent a long burst of fire in the general direction to get the shooter thinking. I only had to keep his head down while Knocker got close.

My magazine ran dry, so I dropped it out and replaced it with a fresh one. I chambered a round and opened fire again.

"I'm almost there, Reaper."

We traded shots for another minute or so before they stopped. A few moments later, Knocker said, "Come on up, Reaper. You're clear."

"Durov?"

"Looking at him."

———

I made my way up to the box and found Knocker standing in the open doorway, M6A2 cradled, staring at Durov, who was sitting in a seat, blood running down the right side of his face from a cut on his cheek. His last bodyguard was lying in the short aisle, dead.

"You're a hard man to catch up with, Durov," I said to him.

He scowled at me. "You have the luck of the devil, Mr. Kane. But just because you kill me, doesn't mean that anything will stop."

"We aren't going to kill you, Misha. We're taking you back to London where some people want to talk to you."

His eyes flickered. "Now, let's get out of here before your friends show up to take you home. Slick, we've got him. Organize an extract."

"Copy, Reaper—shit, you've got incoming. Two SUVs on the street out front."

"Fuck, get him up, Knocker. We need to move."

I led the way out of the balcony box and along the corridor that connected them all. Behind me, Knocker kept shoving Durov forward. The Russian's hands were bound with a zippy tie and blood was still wet on his cheek.

Starting down the stairs, we only got halfway before the first shooter appeared. We opened fire at the same time. His bullets went wide while mine hammered into his torso, knocking him back. I called over my shoulder as a second shooter appeared, "Contact front. Get back up the stairs."

We backpedaled up the stairs to the landing. Covering the others while they climbed, a thought struck me. The attackers weren't worried about who they hit. "Knocker, Durov is the target."

"Shit, roger that."

I blew through the rest of my magazine and killed another of the Russian shooters. Then turned and ran along the hallway toward the far end stairs while reloading. Knocker had already started down the stairs, and took point while I held rear security.

Bullets stitched the wall, blowing holes in wallpaper and drywall. I swung the M6 up and fired a long burst. The legs went from under the shooter, torn to shreds by my rounds. He cried out and fell forward, tumbling toward me.

Raising a foot, I stopped his roll, took out my Glock, and shot him in the head. Glancing up, I saw another shooter appear. The Glock came up and I fired five or six shots, making him pull back.

Then shit turned bad. I took a shot to my chest plate. The impact knocked me backward and I lost my footing, tumbling down the stairs. Knocker stopped me.

"What the bollocks are you doing, Reaper?" he snapped.

"Shut up, I got hit in the plate."

"You all right?" he asked, aiming up the curved staircase. He opened fire before I could answer, so I just climbed painfully to my feet and took point.

At the base of the stairs, I almost ran into another shooter who had cut across from the other side. Reacting quickly, I hit him with the butt of my M6. He reeled back and I shot him as he fell.

"Come on, Knocker."

He appeared with Durov. "Lead the way."

WHAP!

"Fuck!" Knocker exclaimed as he opened fire at a shooter from the stage. "Shit a bloody brick."

The shooter on the stage fell, but I didn't see it. I was too busy looking at Durov. His chest was wet with blood, and he was sinking to his knees. I knelt beside him. "Don't you damn well die on me, you son of a bitch. Not now."

"You are too late, American." He coughed. "This was fated a long time ago."

He grew weaker before my eyes and died.

Just like that, he was snatched from our grasp along with everything he'd held in his mind.

"Did he just die?" Knocker asked, his voice raised. "Don't tell me that fucker didn't just die."

"He's dead," I confirmed.

"Christ on a bloody crutch."

"Move out. Now."

Knocker fired another burst at a Russian shooter, and then we headed for the back door. All the while I could hear him cursing everything that came into his mind. Inwardly, I was doing the same thing.

Out in the lot, Slick was in the driver's seat of the SUV. We piled in and he floored the gas pedal, the tires kicking up gravel as it turned. I looked into the side mirror and saw a handful of shooters appear in the parking lot behind us. But instead of firing, they turned and went back inside.

While we waited for the jet to take us back to London with the diamonds, Slick was still working to see what he could find about the force who'd hit us at the old theater.

"Reaper, have a look at this."

I moved in beside him. Knocker took up position on the other side. We looked down at his computer screen. "This was captured at a small airstrip outside of Antwerp earlier today."

We watched a small business jet taxi to a stop and the stairs were let down. As I counted, twelve men carrying duffels got off the plane. There were no prizes for guessing what they were carrying.

They disappeared from the camera's view and there was a pause before a thirteenth man climbed out. "Can we zoom in on him, Slick?"

The picture adjusted as he zoomed in. "It's not very good. I'll see if I can tidy it up."

His fingers danced across the keyboard and the picture became slightly clearer. "Son of a bitch."

Mikhail Shatov. He'd come himself to make sure there were no mistakes.

"Son of a bitch," I muttered. "Tell me he's still in Antwerp."

"No, the plane left twenty minutes ago."

"Of course, it did," Knocker said. "No prizes for guessing where it went."

"No."

My cell rang.

"Kane."

"Hello, Mr. Kane."

Shatov.

"We were just looking at your picture, Mikhail. Nice

plane you have. Little bit lighter going home. Shame about Durov."

"Misha knew the consequences of what happened. It was rescue or kill, either one sufficed. Too bad it had to be the latter."

"As you say, too bad."

"You sound so confident, Mr. Kane. Maybe you won't be in a few days."

"What's that supposed to mean?" I asked him.

"You will find out. Who was it that said, be careful what you wish for?"

"We're coming for you, Mikhail. One day you'll wake up, and we'll be there."

"Maybe one day, my friend, it will be you who does not wake up."

The call disconnected and I muttered a curse. "He's up to something already."

"So are we, Reaper," Knocker said. "Let's go home."

"*I'm curious,*" *German said.* "*What did you think he was up to?*"

"*We had no idea.*"

"*Not even an inkling of a feeling?*"

"*Nothing.*"

"*None of us had any idea what he was planning to do,*" *Christine Ryan said.*

Holland looked sideways at her. "*I'm beginning to think that you should be on the other side of the table from now on.*"

"*Oh, grow up, Jack,*" *she snapped.* "*Your chauvinism is starting to show. Continue, Mr. Kane. Not long now and we'll call it a day.*"

We were picked up from a small airstrip outside of London by Holly. She was less than impressed, and I could understand that. "What did I say before I fucking left?"

"I have a feeling you're about to tell me."

"I said to stay out of trouble."

I shook my head. "No, I think the word you said was try."

"Same bloody thing. And what happens? You blow up a train."

"Technically, not us."

"Same bloody thing," she repeated. "Put your gear in the back. We've got a meeting with the boss."

As ordered, we put our gear in the rear of the Land Rover before climbing aboard. Holly took us into London proper where we met up with Christine Ryan.

"You mind telling me what the hell happened?" she demanded.

"We had Durov, and his people killed him to keep him quiet. Simple as that."

"Officials in Belgium are screaming at us for the reasons British Intelligence is running an operation in their country without their prior knowledge or approval."

"We don't know who we can trust. Short should have proved that."

"Is that supposed to mean something?" Christine Ryan demanded.

"No, ma'am."

"Tell me what you have."

"Didn't Holly tell you?"

"I want to hear it from you."

"We figure they're building toward something. Oil and money would indicate a war."

"They don't have the capability," Christine Ryan stated bluntly.

"Not yet, ma'am, but give them time. Even though the generals are down from five to four, they're still a formidable organization."

"To start a war would have to go through the Duma."

"The one that just put a hardliner in control of the country?" I asked. "The same Duma that the generals killed members of to replace with their own?"

"I get your point."

There was a knock at the door and a young woman wearing a black pants suit came in holding a piece of paper. She hesitated, and Christine Ryan waved her forward. "Come in, Mary."

"Yes, ma'am."

She handed the paper over and left while it was still being read. Christine Ryan looked up at both of us, worry in her eyes. "Sergey Lash has brought into law that Russia will once again be known as the United Soviet Socialist Republic."

I nodded. "The next part will be them trying to put it back together."

"Don't forget that if they try, they will be going up against NATO."

"For them to get this far, they would have it all planned. They would have to get around the European countries and the US."

"But how?"

"I was hoping Durov could enlighten us on many of those blank spaces."

"What happened to the diamonds you stole from that poor unsuspecting gentleman in Antwerp?"

"They're here along with the others."

"What others?"

"The three suitcases with almost a billion dollars' worth in them."

"Oh, good grief. Get out of my sight. We'll continue this tomorrow."

———

British Intelligence put us up in an apartment in London when we weren't out on missions. While there, we just relaxed, exercised, and watched television. As I flicked through the channels, I stopped on BBC news. It was running a story about Lash and his grand announcement of the new USSR. Knocker sat down and said, "Do you think that this was what Shatov meant when he said about being overconfident?"

"I don't know. Possibly."

"Makes sense if it was. Adds up. It's pretty big."

"Yeah."

But we were wrong. The knock on the door from Holly proved that. I moved across to open it, and she pushed past me into the room, a solemn expression on her face. The news was bad, and I didn't want to ask, but I was drawn to. "What is it?"

"They took Julia Firth."

"Who took her?"

"Shatov's people—I don't know. They filmed her."

"What do you mean, Filmed her?"

"She was tied to a chair. Whoever it was wore masks. They said it was reprisal for what she had done."

"What she had done," Knocker mused. "What the hell did she do?"

I shook my head. "No, this is about us. They're sending us another message. You asked if Shatov meant what Lash did. No, he was referring to Julia."

"They killed her, John. Shot her while she was tied to the chair. They sent the recording to MI6 so we could all see. It was awful to watch."

I put my arm around her. "They always are."

Slick opened the door and walked in. "What's going on?"

Holly burst into tears, unable to hold her composure.

CHAPTER 20

THE BUZZ OF MY CELL TWO DAYS LATER SOUNDED ALMOST urgent. I was in bed. It was early, the sun only just coming up over London, forcing its way through the gray overcast. I grabbed it. "Kane."

No one said a word. The line was dead. "Shit."

I threw it on the bed and lay back. Just as my head hit the pillow the cell started again. This time I was in luck. "Yes?"

"Get in here. We've got something for you and Raymond."

"Holly?"

"Yes."

"What's going on?" I was still half asleep.

"Just get in here, John. You know what, I'll send a car for you both."

"What about Slick?"

"No, just you two."

"All right, I'll wake him up."

I got dressed and went into Knocker's room. He'd been out the night before and brought back some random woman he'd picked up. She was a blonde and had a few tattoos on her body. Her arms and legs were draped across Knocker as she dribbled on his hairy chest.

"She was dribbling on my chest?"

"Yes."

"Bloody hell, no wonder I felt like I'd swam the Channel."

"Gentlemen, please," Christine Ryan said. *"I'd like to get home today."*

I said, "Knocker, get up."

"What?"

"Get up, we have to go to work."

"Already?" he asked with a sigh. He lifted his head and looked at the woman. "Bollocks."

"Get up, Holly's sending a car."

"Yeah, right."

I had coffee waiting for him when he emerged from his room. Handing it to him, I said, "Where did you find her?"

"Ex-girlfriend," he replied. "She used to be a soldier before going to work in sales. Now she—you know, I don't have any idea what she does now."

"Come on, let's go down and wait for our ride."

———

Our chauffeur showed up ten minutes later and we climbed into the SUV he was driving. "Any idea what the flap is about?" Knocker asked.

"No," came the one-word reply.

The rest of the drive was made in silence.

When we arrived, we were shown into a conference room. Holly and another person, a woman we'd never seen before, were waiting for us. "John, Raymond, this is Lisa Goodall. She's our new boss."

"Good morning, gentlemen."

"Ma'am."

"Ma'am."

My assessment of Lisa Goodall was: probably early forties, short blonde hair, athletic build. First impression was that she'd been a field agent at one time. As I found out later, I was right.

There were four folders on the table. We each took one and opened it. Lisa said, "This is Arsen Prutsev. Former KGB back when they were a thing. He wants to come to the UK but is worried that he's being watched."

"Why is he so important?" I asked.

"He says he knows about the generals. Knows what they are up to."

"Did he say what?" Knocker asked.

"No," Holly replied. "That's why we need you to go to Munich and get him out."

"What about family?" I asked.

Lisa said, "Has none. They were killed in a road accident thirty years ago."

"Why does he want to come out?" Knocker asked.

"Does it matter?" Lisa asked.

"It does if my ass is on the line," he replied.

"He could be a wealth of information from back in his KGB days."

"How did he reach out?" I asked.

"Through an old line that was in use in the eighties. It's legitimate. We wouldn't be sending you if it wasn't. The meeting will take place at the Munich Hauptbahnhof. I have one request: Don't blow it up."

"When do we leave?"

"Just as soon as you get on the plane."

———

Touching down in Munich we were taken to a hotel where we checked in. The meeting was scheduled for the following day at the Munich train station. Holly would be in a van outside, and Knocker and I would be inside. We'd take custody of Prutsev and then escort him out before leaving. That was the plan anyway.

The day outside the station was gray, overcast, and wet. Currently it was raining lightly, but the day had brought some showers that had been sharp and heavy. We sat in the van, and I checked my watch. Holly said, "It's almost time."

Picking up our earwigs, we put them in our ears. We did a comms check, weapons check, and then we were ready. "If this is a trap, Holly, and things go wrong, just get out."

"Understood."

Climbing from the van, we splashed through the puddles toward the main entrance. Once inside, we quickly brushed ourselves off and split up, making our way to the RV by circuitous routes.

"Remember, John, he will be next to the Brioche Doree Patisserie," Holly said into my ear. "He'll have a newspaper tucked under his arm and a hat on."

I kept an even stride, trying not to rush, so if need be, I could possibly make out any threats. "Knocker, how's it looking?"

"Looks clear to me, Reaper. You?"

"Same."

I kept walking. A train had just arrived, and a crush of disembarking passengers came toward me. I weaved through them, and ahead of me, I saw the patisserie. Moving left, I took up position near a large pole. I couldn't see Prutsev anywhere.

"Knocker, I'm at the RV. I can't see him."

"Copy, almost there."

"Holly, talk to me."

"I'm trying to get into the feed, Reaper, but I'm having some trouble."

My immediate thought was I wished that Slick was there

instead of in London. I waited, looking around. Still no Prutsev.

"Reaper, I've got him," Knocker said. "He's behind the stand. It's blocking your line of sight."

"Roger that."

I walked forward, feeling the pressure of the Glock I had at the base of my spine. As I rounded the stand I saw him, just as we'd been told he would be. He looked at me and we locked gazes.

"Mr. Prutsev?"

He nodded. "Yes, that's me."

"My name is John, sir. We're here to get you back to London."

He gave me a wan smile and a slight nod. "I never thought I would see the day, but here we are."

"Just follow me, sir. Ray will come along behind us." I looked at Knocker. "You good?"

"Yeah."

WHAP!

Prutsev grunted and started sinking to the cold hard floor. "Christ, Reaper, he's hit."

"Where'd it come from?"

"I don't know."

"Quick, have a look around." I kneeled beside Prutsev. "Holly, Prutsev is down. We need an ambulance. He's been shot."

"Oh, no."

I ripped the Russian's shirt open and saw the wound in his chest. I tried to stanch the flow of blood, but it wouldn't stop. Already he was turning gray, and his eyes were glassy. "Hang in there, Arsen. Stay with me, help is coming."

"They—they have killed me."

"Who, Arsen? Who has killed you?" I asked.

"Can y-you hear me?"

"I can hear you."

"S-Stalin's Spear. You must stop it. Tell—tell me you will."

"What is Stalin's Spear, Arsen?"

He mumbled something incoherent.

"What was that?"

But he was gone. "Holly, Arsen is gone. He's dead."

"Damn it."

"Can you see anything?"

"No—wait. I have someone leaving the building through the main entrance and running to the parking lot."

"On my way. Knocker, out front."

"Coming."

I hated leaving Prutsev, but the man was dead. Running back outside, we found Holly waiting for us. We jumped into the van, me in the passenger seat, Knocker in the back. Holly said, "The assassin got into a BMW and hot-footed it out of the parking lot. Did you get a look at him?"

"Not even a brief look."

The van leaned wildly as it took a sharp corner. We caught a glimpse of the BMW at the end of the street, turning left. Holly slammed on the brakes at a pedestrian crossing loaded with people.

"Bloody drive over them," Knocker growled.

Holly blasted her horn and started forward, pedestrians scattering. Some shouting abuse at the impatient driver. "Did Prutsev say anything?"

"Stalin's Spear," I replied.

"What's that?"

"I don't know. Before he died, he just said that and asked me to stop it."

Holly braked hard once more before making the left turn. The rear of the van skipped on the damp street before snapping into line as she corrected the skid. She floored the gas pedal, and the van seemed to groan as it picked up pace.

"Tell me why we're in this bloody turtle?" Knocker grumbled.

"I wasn't planning on a car chase through the streets of bloody Munich," Holly spat.

She swerved onto the wrong side of the street around a vehicle in front before cutting back into the correct lane, almost running head-on into an Audi coming the other way.

I hung onto the door handle, my body swaying left and right with the motion of the van swerving. Traffic had slowed the BMW in front and it was now three vehicles ahead. He must have caught sight of us because the vehicle swerved out into oncoming traffic, forcing the drivers to veer wildly and crash.

Holly let out a curse and wrestled the wheel. She managed to miss a Mercedes and squeezed through a narrow gap through which the van shouldn't have been able to fit. And it didn't—not really, because a side mirror was knocked off and a scraping sound screeched from the left side.

It made me wince as the sound pierced my ears. Knocker said, "Damn, there goes a coat of paint. I think that was a new BMW."

"Can't help it if he can't bloody drive," Holly growled. Her foot went down hard on the brake pedal, and I slammed against the seatbelt strap. "Fuck! Get out of the way!"

"That's it, girl," Knocker said. "You tell them."

Holly saw a gap.

Floored the gas pedal.

And crashed through, the sound of crunching panels and fenders reaching my ears. "There," she said, "I knew we could fit."

She started swerving, honking the horn, and cutting drivers off. Suddenly Holly had become like a road demon.

All that was missing were the flames and skulls on the front.

The BMW we were chasing turned right and disappeared into an alley. Holly followed it and ran right into its rear.

"Shit," I grunted and threw the door open. I ran forward to the driver's window and saw that the vehicle was empty. "Damn it."

I looked around to see where the driver had gone. Saw nothing. He couldn't have just disappeared. But he had. I slammed my hand down onto the BMW's roof and cursed our luck. Several times.

"He's gone."

"He can't just disappear," Holly said.

"Well, he has," I said. "And so should we. Come on."

———

We flew back to London empty-handed. The debriefing was short. We didn't know the assassin, nor did we know what Stalin's Spear was.

Knocker and I were angry at the outcome. We'd lost people and still had no definitive answer as to what they were up to. Sure, we could guess, but that would get us nowhere.

We met with Lisa Goodall, who was less than impressed. "You lot made me look like a damn fool."

"Wasn't us," Knocker retorted. "You did that all on your own."

"I beg your pardon?"

"Leave it, Raymond," Holly cautioned him.

"Whatever."

"There is an election looming, and all of this attention isn't good. The Prime Minister has enough on his plate. We can't have it blowing up. If it does, you personally will be giving a leg up to the opposition leader. And trust me, if he gets into power, the country will go down the toilet." Lisa sighed. "You can all take a few days while we figure out what to do next. When you return, I have something else you can do while we're working on the problem."

"Shoveling snow in Greenland?" Knocker asked.

"No. Since you two are so adept at death and destruction wherever you go, I'm going to send you to Mexico."

I frowned. "What is in Mexico?"

"Someone who is classed as a threat to national security. Someone we want you to kill."

"Who?"

"You'll be given the information before you leave." Lisa collected the papers in front of her and stood up. "That's all."

———

While we regrouped in London, Shatov was holding another meeting with his remaining generals. He was far from happy. We'd cost him Durov and we knew about Noskov, which kept us in the game for him. But there were still two others who were yet to cross our paths, and we had no idea what they looked like.

He looked at the empty seat and said, "We have a vacancy at the table. These people are becoming tiresome. Before we move on, I want a concerted effort made to eliminate them."

"Let me do it, Mikhail," Noskov said.

"No, I have other work for you to do here." He turned to a man on his left. "Can you handle it?"

The general nodded. "I can, but it might get messy."

"Get as messy as you want. I do not care. I want them out of the way. We still have more preparations to make before Stalin's Spear can be executed."

"You can rely on me, Mikhail."

"I hope so. Just let me know what you need, and I'll provide it for you."

A door opened and two men in suits walked in, followed by a third. All the generals who weren't standing came to their feet. Mikhail said, "President Lash, we weren't expecting you."

"I'm just checking in to see how things are progressing, Mikhail."

"We've had our share of hiccups, sir. We have lost Misha."

"I'm sorry to hear that."

"Thank you, sir. We are about to enter a new phase, but first, we have some things to tidy up."

Lash looked around the room. He nodded slowly. "Dolos?"

"He is ready."

"And the missiles?"

"Almost to their destination," Shatov said.

"Good. When my father was made Marshal of the Soviet Union, it was one of his proudest achievements."

"I remember," Shatov said.

Lash said, "I now bestow that same rank upon you, Mikhail. I see no one more deserving than you. What you have given up for the motherland has been extraordinary. Now it gives something back."

"I-I don't know what to say, Comrade President."

"Say nothing, Mikhail. Just keep serving your country as you have done and all will be fine. Now I must go. Good luck, Mikhail."

"Thank you, Comrade President."

The last man through the door closed it behind him, and the three generals turned to Marshal of the Soviet Union Shatov and started clapping.

Shatov's only worry was living up to the expectation that had just been bestowed upon him.

Christine Ryan sighed. "I think that will do for today. Tomorrow, we'll move on to Berlin."

Berlin was a shit show.

"I can't wait," Holland said, his voice laced with sarcasm.

"Before we go," German said. "What were your thoughts about things at this point in time?"

I glanced at Knocker and Holly. Knocker shrugged. Holly nodded. I said, "We were getting close. What happened next proved that. It was an all-out attack on their behalf. They turned Berlin into a war zone."

"Don't get into it now," Christine Ryan said. "Save the details for tomorrow or we'll be here all night. Be back here the same time in the morning."

———

Leaving our interrogation room, we stopped on the steps outside the building. I let out a long breath, feeling weary.

Holly said, "Who wants a beer?"

Strangely enough, Knocker shook his head. "Sorry, I'm catching up with an old friend. And, no, it isn't a woman."

"John?"

I looked at her and nodded. "Sure, why not?"

"Don't be late home, Reaper. Or call if you're going to be out all night."

"Yes, mom."

Knocker disappeared around the corner and Holly asked, "How do you figure today went?"

"Crap. Tomorrow is going to be worse."

"Do you think they believe us?"

I shrugged. "I guess we'll find out in the end."

A LOOK AT BOOK THREE:
STALIN'S SPEAR

Kane and Jensen must stop Berlin's secrets from igniting the next global firestorm...

In the shadowed streets of Berlin, an urgent call from an old ally spirals into a deadly trap. As Kane, Jensen, and their elite team navigate through the maze of treachery, they find themselves ensnared in a sinister plot decades in the making. At the heart of this conspiracy pulses Stalin's Spear, a Cold War relic rekindled to unleash global nuclear chaos.

As the city's air crackles with looming peril, it becomes clear that the Gods of War are behind the mayhem. Driven by dark ambitions, they weave their diabolical schemes, pushing humanity toward an unthinkable brink.

Kane and Jensen must decode the shadows of the past to thwart a catastrophe that threatens to consume the present. Can they dismantle Stalin's Spear before it ignites the world?

Dive into this thrilling espionage adventure where every shadow holds a secret and every ally could be an enemy.

AVAILABLE AUGUST 2024

ABOUT THE AUTHOR

A relative newcomer to the world of writing, Brent Towns self-published his first book in 2015. Last Stand in Sanctuary took him two years to write. His first hardcover book, a Black Horse Western, was published the following year.

Since then, he has written twenty-six western stories, including some in collaboration with British western author, Ben Bridges; several action adventure novels, such as his bestselling Team Reaper series; the novelization to the 2019 movie, Bill Tilghman and the Outlaws; as well as scripted a handful of Commando Comics. Not bad for an Australian author, he thinks.

Often up until the small hours of the night, bashing away at his tortured keyboard in Queensland, Australia, Brent loves to lose himself in the world of fiction. If you're interested in sharing your thoughts in more detail, scan the QR code below! Your feedback is invaluable to him—and often helps shape his future writing endeavors.